A MATCH FOR
LADY CONSTANCE

A MATCH FOR LADY CONSTANCE

•

Judith Lown

AVALON BOOKS
NEW YORK

Published by Thomas Bouregy & Co., Inc.
160 Madison Avenue, New York, NY 10016

PRINTED IN THE UNITED STATES OF AMERICA
ON ACID-FREE PAPER
BY HADDON CRAFTSMEN, BLOOMSBURG, PENNSYLVANIA

To John

Chapter One

I cannot explain satisfactorily to myself, much less to anyone else, the cause of my appalling lack of common sense that evening during the last week of April, in the Year of our Lord 1816. It was the beginning of my fifth season, and Mama and I were once more facing a London spring with differing, if not actually conflicting purposes. Mama continued to believe, in spite of all evidence to the contrary, that my fondest wish was to become betrothed to a gentleman of the highest possible standing and fortune. Although I had no objection to such a goal per se, my requirements in a spouse were more exacting. Until I could find a gentleman as blind to my faults, indulgent of my whims, and supremely concerned with my happiness as my dear parents had always shown themselves to be, I saw no reason to compromise my carefree life as their adored youngest child and only daughter.

Since before my triumphant come-out the spring of my eighteenth year, when I had been unanimously recognized as an Incomparable, Mama had entered each season fully expecting me to have a choice of eligible bridegrooms. To her astonishment, no serious suitor had applied to my father, Lord Chase, for my hand. True, there were fashionable fribbles and gazetted fortune hunters who had nerved themselves for the interview, but not one candidate from Mama's annual list of eligibles had applied for the demanding task of becoming my husband.

My heretofore indomitable mother had taken to her chaise longue in a decline after my previous season, unable to account for the fact that Lady Constance Hatton, her only daughter and possessor of a generous dowry, a respected and noble name, a spotless reputation, a halo of sun-gold curls, forget-me-not eyes, porcelain rose complexion, a swanlike neck—one blushes to continue—inexplicably had not made a splendid match.

I admit to feeling some pity for her as she emerged from her debilitated state, and not unlike the intrepid Wellington at Waterloo, once again, began to marshal her forces for one final grand assault upon the Marriage Mart. Even Mama, mistress of five large estates, organizer *non pareil* of endless dinners, routs, levees, musicales, and balls, could not be expected to achieve her most cherished dream with a traitor in the ranks, namely her much loved and only daughter. For while Mama was busy discovering potential husbands for me, I was testing their devotion and finding them wanting.

I had not begun my social career at odds with my dear mother's purposes. Indeed, as an eager eighteen-year-old, I too had expected to crown a successful season with a wreath of orange blossoms. Perhaps, had I been less of a toast—had fewer odes been dedicated to my eyes, my cheek, my locks, my grace, or whatever, had I been less constantly surrounded by a crush of eager swains who gathered about me at every ball, I might have accepted the gentlemen's attentions with greater appreciation.

But then, as it became clear to me that I would be receiving upwards of five offers from essentially indistinguishable distinguished heirs to honorable houses and fortunes, I realized that I had no basis whatsoever to choose one from the other. Furthermore, I strongly suspected that had some other young miss been given the nod as the match of the season, I would not have received much notice from any one of them. It was this realization that set me on the course I was still pursuing. My first, and each year since, I had eluded every suitor on Mama's list of eligibles. Indeed, I had accomplished this with such skill, each one thought that his attention had been captured by another damsel, a young lady who believed she had stolen Lady Constance Hatton's intended, only hours before Lord Chase was to have been addressed.

Obviously, if one looks for inadequacies in gentlemen, it is not difficult to find them. The handsome, well set up gentleman will unfailingly reveal that he secretly believes his beloved to be the most fortunate of ladies to receive his attentions. The exceptionally rich suitor will subtly reveal his conviction that his loved one's affection and obedience can be bought. And those who possess both attributes, possess both faults.

As I continued to assess my admirers' potential to become a life's companion unfailingly adoring and indulgent of my own self, their shortcomings became so immediately apparent, I rarely considered for very long if Lord X or Mr. Y would be an acceptable husband. As soon as a gentleman began to court me, I began to canvass the ranks of the newest crop of young misses for one to throw across his pathway. Of course, each year there were fewer suitors for me to contend with and the choice of alternative brides became younger and younger. Mama was desperate.

After our arrival in the metropolis, she wasted no time in compiling a list of eligibles, which, although never committed to writing, nevertheless quickly became engraved upon my brain, as had their antecedents. Mercifully, these lists had become shorter over the years, or else, who knows what vital information would have had to be discarded from my thinking apparatus in order to accommodate the full pedigrees, properties, and annual incomes of the very crème of single British manhood. Initially, Mama went about the task of considering, deleting and adding to this year's list with an air more of perseverance than enthusiasm. But the day she learned Lord Bamwell had returned to society with the intention of finding a bride, her spirits rose noticeably. My own fell markedly.

Lord Bamwell had been at the top of Mama's first list five

years previously. A tall, large-boned, florid-faced man, said to be a bruising rider—his horse would agree, I imagine—had favored me with a most energetic country dance, an "honored, honored, don't ya know" and, to my relief, decided to pursue Lady Frances Coxhampton whose dowry included property adjoining Lord Bamwell's principal seat. The only controversy ever to have been attached to Lady Frances was whether "mousey" or "rabbitty" more accurately described her appearance.

The poor creature had presented her lord with three daughters in three years of marriage, and had expired shortly after the birth of the third. Lord Bamwell, his year of mourning over, his enlarged estate under reliable management, had come to town to find a new bride, a mother for his three young daughters, and—he obviously hoped—a mother to bear an heir. Mama was planning a charge. I began to plan a strategic retreat.

I had no premonition on that chilly April evening, as I sat in the carriage inching its way to the portals of Sir Nigel and Lady Sandforth's town house for the come-out ball of their daughter, Althea, that my life was soon to take a quite unexpected turn. The only difference between that evening and all the evenings immediately preceding, was Papa's choosing to accompany Mama and me, a favor that important government business usually forbade.

My esteemed, and still handsome parents sat opposite me as we made our slow progress. Mama, whose blue eyes mirrored my own, and whose greyed blond hair was all but obscured by a deep blue turban exactly matched to the blue of her gown and the sapphires which sparkled at her throat and ears, endeavored to inform Papa of all the *on dits* that he should know in order to avoid uttering an unfortunate word in the wrong direction. To me, it was clear that Papa's occasional "hmm" and "I see" and "in truth" bore no relationship to Mama's points of information, but nothing he said or did not say staunched the flow of her briefing.

Eventually we were deposited at the Sandforth's door,

where we joined still another line which inched its way up a grand stairway to the place where we would bow or curtsey to our hosts and then be free to pursue the evening's entertainment: Mama to the ranks of chaperones' gossip, Papa to serious discussions with other distinguished gentlemen, and perhaps a hand or two of whist, and I to the scene of conflict, the dance floor.

As usual, my dance card was quickly filled, and I was pleased to be able to limit Lord Bamwell to one entry. He was becoming quite presumptuously proprietary in his attitude toward me, and I was determined to deny him the two dances that official suitors routinely claimed. But to my dismay, as he made his ponderous way to my side, the unmistakable strains of the waltz wafted across the room.

He beamed at me, winked with the subtlety of an ox, and "whispered" for the edification of half the ballroom, that he had "crossed the palm of the conductor chap with a little gold, don't ya know" so that we could share a waltz, which to his thinking, only my dizzy little female brain had prevented me from saving for him in the first place.

I do not mean to minimize the gallantry and courage of the men of our army and navy, but I do believe that ladies are also called upon to display a unique sort of courage when faced with a dance partner such as Lord Bamwell. He grasped me in a firm, moist grip and, setting his rounded jaw and chin in purposeful manner, proceeded to steer me—forward for him, backward for me—in great, long strides. It was as if someone had shouted "Charge!"

Now, I am no slight, fragile miss. Indeed, Mama believes that my five-feet-seven inch height may very well be the tragic flaw that has left me unclaimed. But, that I stayed on my feet for the duration of the "waltz" with Lord Bamwell can be attributed only to my excellent sense of balance, exceptionally fine coordination, four years of intensive ballroom experience, and the happy coincidence of flat ballroom slippers being in fashion.

Under the circumstances, I believe it was no act of cowardice that, immediately after I rose from my curtsey at the conclusion of my ordeal, I fled the scene of action. I purposely did not retire to the room set aside for ladies to repair their garments and persons. I wanted not only to assess needed repairs, but also to find a place of quiet seclusion where I could gather my wits and devise a quick and successful campaign that would shift Lord Bamwell's ardor to some other eligible creature.

I made my way down a dim corridor, and seeing light under a door on my left, put my ear to it. Hearing no voices, I cautiously opened the door. I entered what appeared to be a library for someone who did not care much for reading. Indeed, no one had ever accused a Sandforth of being bookish. There were three small but exquisite book cases containing volumes elegantly bound in a rich maroon leather, which exactly matched maroon flowers featured in the heavy damask curtains and the background of the soft carpet. To my left was a lighted fireplace with an ornately carved mantle. Two sofas flanked the hearth so their occupants could converse while enjoying the fire.

On the wall opposite the fireplace was a looking glass perfectly suited to my needs. Candle sconces on either side of the glass afforded me the opportunity to check for the damages I was certain my carefully constructed, carefree hairdo had suffered during the rigors of the evening's dancing. But just as I had tucked back a stray ribbon, I heard the soft click of the door being opened. My first thought was that Bamwell had followed me, and I would not have put it past my scheming Mama to be waiting just long enough to find us in a "compromising" situation. I ducked behind a maroon-flowered damask curtain and prayed.

How long I stood with closed eyes, not wanting to breathe, I could not say. But a whiff of smoke caused me to open my eyes in alarm as I tried desperately to stifle the need to sneeze, a need that became more urgent with each passing second.

"Guinea-gold hair, cornflower blue eyes, wide smiling

mouth, and the trimmest ankles in Christendom. It must be Lady Constance Hatton."

The voice was masculine, but not Lord Bamwell's.

I felt my face flame with embarrassment over the impertinent references to my person, and reflexively glanced down in the darkness of my hiding place to check if perhaps my ankles were somehow exposed. There was not sufficient light for me to see my feet, much less my ankles. I knew a moment of wanting to remain in my hiding place, like a small child who believes that if she cannot see, she cannot be seen. But I took a deep breath and looked out from behind the curtain.

A man, dressed all in black and white eveningwear of the finest cut and cloth was leaning against the side of the mantle. His hair was black. His eyes were black. His face was harsh and tanned. He was holding the cause of my need to sneeze: a cigar, from which smoke curled lazily toward the cherubs cavorting on the ceiling.

Without thinking I began to protest.

"You could not possibly have seen . . ." and stopped in embarrassed confusion. I had been about to repeat the rogue's improper reference to my person, a lapse I would have known better than to have committed in my first season. I hoped he would not observe my blush in the subdued light.

"Of course your remarkable ankles are well-hidden, under multiple layers, one assumes. But one golden curl remaining outside the curtain was the only hint needed to your identity. Given that one golden curl, the complete, charming picture sprang immediately to mind."

He smiled, which transformed his daunting visage into attractive geniality.

The occasion called for a witty but stinging set-down for his impertinence and a speedy exit from the room. Yet any rejoinder eluded me, and I remained as if glued to the spot where I was standing, looking out from behind the curtain like some green country miss. When had I ever been inca-

pable of finding words to arrest easy flattery that threatened
to become too warm? Wide mouth! Trim ankles! A gentleman never offered such compliments to a lady. But a sophisticated rebuke did not materialize. A sneeze did. A fresh
man-sized handkerchief was thrust into my hand.

"Excuse me, sir—my lord—the dust from the curtain, no
doubt," I managed in my most repressive tones, glaring at
the offending cigar, pleased that my skill at verbal combat
had returned.

A proper gentleman would have apologized profusely after tossing the cigar into the fire. This insufferable man responded by returning the cigar to his mouth, inhaling deeply
and slowly expelling a stream of smoke in the direction of
the cherubs, who would more resemble chimney sweeps by
the end of the evening. All the while he continued to gaze at
me with what can only be described as amused assessment.

"Forgive me for not introducing myself. Blaise de
Grenault, at your service, Lady Constance."

He executed a fluid bow.

I did not offer him my hand. I had scarcely been able to
keep my wits about me since the beginning of this absurd
conversation. I did not care to imagine the effect of the
man's touch, even through my evening glove. Of course I
had known instantly who he was, although he had never
been formally presented to me in the five years since my
come-out.

"Blaise de Grenault" he had called himself. He was the
Marquis de Rochmont, regardless of his cavalier attitude toward his title. He was an émigré who had not settled into the
genteel poverty and mourning expected of those fortunate
enough to have escaped The Terror with their heads attached
to their shoulders. Instead, and in spite of constant warfare,
he had pursued commerce over four or five continents and
was known to be as rich as Midas. He was also known to
chase beautiful widows and neglected wives. He was for-
given his pursuit of women. His pursuit of commerce, when
it resulted in an astonishing fortune, was ignored. The *ton*,

fashionable society, chose to remember his ancient title and gave him entree into the highest circles.

But careful mamas had assessed him as being "too foreign" and, no doubt "unreliable", that is, not at all malleable, and, in spite of his riches, had excluded him from the ranks of eligibles. Apparently that state of affairs suited him as well as it did the mamas. For, to my very extensive knowledge, he had never shown the slightest hint of interest in the endless parade of debutantes who were part of the larger circle within which he moved with ease.

He most certainly had never been on one of my own dear Mama's lists of prospective husbands for me. Nor had he qualified for her "to be avoided" lists of second sons with no prospects and fortune hunters from impoverished noble families. She simply had never conceived of the remotest possibility that I would have occasion for more than a perfunctory exchange with him. Common sense dictated that I flee the room.

"No need to go running off."

No wonder Lord Rochmont was so successful in commerce. The man was a mind reader. He favored me once more with his memorable smile. I could have sworn his eyes twinkled. How could eyes as black as sin twinkle? He motioned toward the door with his cigar, dropping ash on the carpet. I barely resisted the urge to stamp on the ash with my slippered toe, a move that would have brought me into even closer and more uncomfortable proximity to the marquis. He evidently read my thoughts once more, for a small flicker of amusement crossed his face.

"You must have just made good your escape from the estimable Bamwell. The man's a menace in the ballroom. Should be forbidden the waltz. You are to be commended upon your survival."

Without thinking, I collapsed onto a sofa and dissolved into laughter.

"Oh dear!" I exclaimed, as I straightened my back, checked that I was perched properly on the very edge of the cushion, and wiped my streaming eyes. "Mama despairs of what she calls my 'unseemly ebullience'."

"Ah, your mother, the redoubtable Lady Chase. So aptly named too. Master, or should I say Mistress of the Hunt. 'Tallyho!' And all eligible gentlemen attend her cry, pursuing the clever vixen, who year after year eludes them all and continues to run free."

I was struck by his interpretation of my "unsuccessful" seasons.

"What a novel way of looking at things. It quite lifts my spirits, to be thought of as the pursued rather than the pursuer."

A perspective, I did not add, which agreed perfectly with my own.

"But of course," Lord Rochmont explained patiently. "Just look at the numbers. Clearly, the hunters of Lady Chase's pack are your suitors. You are no hunter. What sort of hunter lets the quarry go time and again? How many offers have you refused or avoided, Lady Constance?"

"Lord Rochmont!" I knew my protest was useless, but habit and training do not disappear just because they are irrelevant. "However would you learn of such matters? I assure you, I keep anything of such a personal nature in strictest confidence."

"And usually provide an alternative bride for your rejected swain. Stunning strategy, my dear Lady Constance. And quite profitable for me too."

My bewilderment must have shown on my face. The marquis lifted his eyebrows in amazement at my failure to understand what he was saying.

"The betting books, Lady Constance. I have not seen them yet this year, but no sooner is Lady Chase's list discerned, the odds of your betrothal to each gentleman are established. I bet against them all. Have not lost yet. Then there are the side bets on the matches you arrange. Why no one sees your manipulations is beyond me. But I do not complain. I have made a tidy bundle over the last four years, thanks to you."

He sketched a bow and drew deeply on the cigar.

I suddenly felt quite weary. It must have been memories of four years of frustrating Mama's plans and acting as matchmaker for so many would-be mates. I sighed deeply and wiggled my aching toes.

"Poor Lady Constance." He sounded sincere and somehow comforting. Skills no doubt perfected comforting widows and neglected wives. "Do not tell me you are tiring of your game! It is not just winning wagers that gives me pleasure, don't you see—it is also the sight of the vixen escaping the pack."

The man was a puzzle to be sure. I decided it was my turn to ask an impertinent question.

"How in heaven's name is it that you speak such faultless English? Not only your accent, but the words you use too. When you said, 'It is not just winning wagers, don't you see,'—why any one of my brothers might express himself just so."

Rochmont laughed and threw his cigar stub into the fire.

"A tousan pardon, my ladee. I am desole to disappoint so ravishment a creature."

He had become the incarnation of an English caricature of a Frenchman. In a second he changed back to his original persona of Englishman. A wry smile twisted his mouth as he gazed into the fire—longing for his discarded cigar or seeing some private memory, I could not tell.

"Let me assure you, Lady Constance, that the finest instruction in a new language does not come from a tutor. It comes from young boys who delight in making life a penance for a strange foreign being who arrives in their midst speaking some incomprehensible babble and gesturing in ways that provide them with endless entertainment. I landed on these pleasant shores at ten years of age. My instruction in the English language and all things English was so successful, that by my twelfth birthday, I daresay only my appearance betrayed my foreign origins."

Never before had I felt the slightest inclination to apologize for English behavior, which had always seemed to me to be clearly superior to that of any other country. But in my mind's eye, I saw a small, dark, perhaps ragged, refugee boy having lost home and family to unspeakable horrors, being taunted unmercifully by spoiled scions of the English upper class.

Tears filled my eyes, and as I dabbed at them with the handkerchief Lord Rochmont had provided me, I endeavored to express my regret for the want of feeling on the part of my young countrymen.

"What a perfectly dreadful . . ." I choked out.

But my sympathy was misplaced. The marquis laughed until his shoulders shook.

"How charming to find a tender heart in such a devious schemer. How tempting to draw out a story of pain and misery. I wonder, if I were moved to tears by my own story, would you dry them for me?"

As he spoke, he poured a glass of brandy and sat down beside me on the sofa.

I now know that if my mental faculties had been functioning efficiently, I would have run from the room. In my own defense, all I can plead is total exhaustion. In a brief time, I had experienced anger, fear, laughter, tears, and a good bit of confusion. To be utterly candid, I also had never been so entertained.

After offering me a glass of brandy, which I retained sufficient sense to refuse, Rochmont settled himself comfortably, sipping his drink, then placing it on a small nearby table. Casually, he draped his right arm along the back of the sofa. Only the fact that I remained perched on the very edge of the seat, hands folded tightly in my lap, as if speaking with the vicar, prevented me from being in his embrace. He gave no indication of noticing my discomfort.

"No need to waste your tears on my account, dear lady. What I learned then was that I have quite an extraordinary, and I must say, very useful facility in language. Always helps to make oneself understood by the natives, washed or unwashed."

He picked up his glass, saluted me with it, and replaced it on the table, never taking his eyes from mine. Somehow in the process, he had moved closer to me, and to my consternation, I saw that his knee was less than an inch from my own. My heart began to pound. I felt much more like a hare with a hawk descending on it than a vixen running free.

He gently unfolded my clasped hands, and continued discussing his linguistic accomplishments.

"So I speak any number of languages, and many varieties of English: the King's, East End, Coastal Sussex."

He counted them off my fingers as one might count guests invited to a small dinner party. "But Debutante," he played idly with my ring finger, "Debutante is one variety of English that I have yet to master."

He leaned forward, kissing me lightly on the lips. I heard a soft click. What was this man doing to disorder my senses so? But my senses were not disordered. What I had heard was the sound of the door being opened. The next thing I knew, Lord Rochmont was on his feet, bowing to Papa, who stood framed in the doorway.

"Lord Chase," the marquis was saying, "may I do myself the honor of calling on you tomorrow to seek your permission to ask your daughter, Lady Constance, to become my wife?"

Papa neither looked at me nor hesitated before answering, "About half past two, if that is convenient."

Chapter Two

The next morning I awoke to the determined trilling of a bluebird outside my bedroom window. Bright sunshine penetrated the curtains. Daisy, my maid, taking a cue from the bluebird, treated me to a steady stream of bright chatter as she made her way to my bed with a cup of tea.

"It's a glorious day, my lady, if I say so myself, and I do say so. I promise you that spring has arrived at last. I don't think I need to even bother throwing any more coal on the fire this morning, indeedy not. Now here's you a nice hot cup o' tea with lemon, just like you like it. Although, if it gets any warmer, you might be wantin' some lemonade instead, though that might be just a bit too sweet so early in the morning, come to think of it. Let me plump those pillows and get a bed jacket for your shoulders. Even with the weather so fine, there's always the chance of an odd draft. Pr'haps I should throw a bit of coal on the fire, what think you, my lady, and how about I set out that new muslin dress with them perty little blue flowers on it that you haven't worn yet since Madame Yvette sent it over last week . . . Lands! My lady, you're looking that peaked, you are! Are you sickenin' for somethin'? I'll fetch Lady Chase right away."

"Thank you, no, Daisy, I am absolutely fine." An outright lie, but I could not face Mama before a cup of tea and some time to compose my thoughts.

14

"And I shall wear the lavender silk, I believe."

I was feeling too much like a young miss just out of the schoolroom; I feared the sprigged muslin would make me look like one too, in spite of Madame Yvette's sophisticated styling.

This was Daisy's first trip to London. Her older sister, Primrose, or Prim, as I had dubbed her when we were both seventeen and she became my maid, had succumbed to the importuning of Nat Carver, the descendant of generations of farmers attached to Hatton Court, the principal seat of the Earls of Chase. Before becoming Mrs. Nat Carver, Prim had asked that I take her younger sister as her replacement, and I was happy to do so as a favor to a maid who had been a loyal friend. It also helped me avoid the appointment of that superior type of female dresser favored by London employment agencies, invariably named "Judson" or "Thomkins", who reserve the right to censure their employers' standards. It never would have occurred to freckle-faced, flame-haired, flat-chested Daisy to offer one syllable of criticism of me. But such devotion, I was discovering, had its price.

As I sipped my tea, I reviewed the events of the previous evening.

Somehow, I had managed to reenter the ballroom, make excuses for "a touch of vertigo", nod and smile at my partners, and make my feet move in the appropriate steps. All the while, I detected a look on Mama's face that let me know I would have to answer for my extended absence from the dance floor.

I was not disappointed. As soon as she, Papa, and I settled ourselves for the carriage ride home, she launched her interrogation.

"Constance, my love, I was not surprised that you wanted time to compose yourself after your turn with Lord Bamwell. Flattering as his attentions are, I am sure that in his enthusiasm, he forgets such marked preference before a formal betrothal is a little overwhelming for a lady of delicate sensibilities. But when you did not return and had left two partners bereft, I sought you out in the ladies' with-drawing room and discovered, to my astonishment, not only were you not there, no one could recall your having been there! My dear, I pride myself on your total discretion. In-deed, I know of no other mother who can depend so com-pletely on her daughter to avoid situations that raise embarrassing questions. But you did miss four dances and most of supper. Whatever were you doing?"

"She was in the library, Honoria, no doubt engaged in dis-cussion of a literary nature."

Something in Papa's deceptively mild tone told me I could not depend on him to keep my secret.

The dim light in the carriage kept me from seeing the look of horror that I was certain was on Mama's face.

"Constance! How could you!" she cried. "You know quite well, for I have told you from your girlhood, that there is nothing so off-putting to gentlemen in search of a wife as the hint of the bluestocking in a prospective bride! Atten-dance at a tasteful poetry reading is quite unexceptionable. Indeed, it reassures a gentleman of a lady's refinement of mind. But a bookish discussion during a ball! How distress-ing! I can scarcely credit that you would so forget yourself as to take part in such an eccentric activity."

She gripped Papa's arm, and in subdued tones gave voice to what she believed were her worst fears. "Julian, you don't think that our Constance will turn out like your Aunt Matilda?"

My Great Aunt Matilda's independence of mind and con-duct are legend in the Hatton family. Mama made light of her eccentricities whenever they were discussed outside the family, but from earliest childhood, I had perceived that the lanky, outspoken lady who never shied away from answer-ing my most inconvenient questions, was not to be consid-ered an acceptable model for my life's course.

"No need to fret, m'dear," Papa patted the white-knuckled hand clutching his arm.

I was stunned. Never had I suspected my father of such

deviousness. Surely what he knew to be the truth would overset Mama even more than the idea that I might have inclinations toward unfeminine intellectual pursuits. And I was certain he was preparing to impart the truth to her.

"I doubt any report that our Connie is a budding bluestocking is likely to circulate. There was, by my firsthand and very close observation, but one other member of our daughter's discussion group, and he is known for his ability to keep a secret."

Papa's matter of fact tone lulled Mama into a false sense of reassurance. She relaxed her hold on his arm and settled back in her seat before the full import of what he had said struck her. I knew the instant it registered, for she sat bolt upright, turning to him, once more gripping his arm. If he suffered bruises, it was what he deserved, for he was playing both Mama and me like the trout that he loves to angle.

"He?" Mama's voice was so faint, I could scarcely recognize it as hers. "Our Constance was alone in the library with a gentleman for the duration of four dances?"

"And part of supper too," Papa added, once more patting the fingers that clutched at him. "But, you will be happy to know that the demanding task of finding a husband for our daughter is about to end in success. Tomorrow at half past two, I am expecting formal application for her hand from her companion in the library, Blaise de Grenault, Lord Rochmont."

For the first time in my life, I saw my indomitable mother search frantically through her evening bag for her smelling salts in order to apply them to her own refined nose. Always before, she had carried smelling salts for others, of weaker disposition.

It was the one mercy of the disastrous evening that at that precise moment, the carriage stopped at Hatton House, and no further conversation was necessary as servants helped us out of the carriage, through the portal of our domicile, and up the stairs to our respective bedrooms.

* * *

My memories of the previous evening's debacle were interrupted by Daisy's return. She brought with her new concerns. She informed me that Lady Chase was still abed and intended to remain there because of a severe headache, and that Lord Chase requested my presence in his study at my earliest convenience.

Poor, innocent Daisy thought she was reassuring me when she said, "Not to worry, my lady, I'm sure that her ladyship will be right as rain before long and eager to go out on calls with you to catch up on all the gossip. And Lord Chase just might have news of a handsome suitor. Oh, my lady, just think how thrilling! You a bride!" She placed her hand over her heart responding to what appeared to be a holy vision.

A handsome suitor indeed! The unrelieved angles of Lord Rochmont's countenance appeared in my mind's eye as did his unreadable eyes and his cool, detached manner. I had not out-schemed Mama for all these years to be chained for life to a man whose warmest regard for me was mild amusement. I had to convince Papa to let me off with a caution about the dangers of flouting society's rules.

I longed to dawdle over my toilette, but I knew that "at my earliest convenience" from Papa meant "at *his* earliest convenience", which translated into "immediately". I did change my mind about my gown, much to Daisy's satisfaction. I chose the muslin with "them perty blue flowers". Perhaps if I looked like a schoolroom miss, Papa would be more kindly disposed toward me.

He did not glance up as I responded to his "enter" when I knocked on the study door. He was evidently finishing a missive that was of more importance to him than the tranquility of his one and only daughter. I gazed about the room as I waited. Usually, being in my father's inner sanctum with its walnut paneling and deep colors bestowed upon me the feeling of absolute security. Papa, along with Grandpapa and Great Grandpapa, whose portraits looked down upon me solemnly, were men of unquestioned power, and I had always felt their power as protection and the guarantor that my life would proceed smoothly, very much to my own liking.

But on that morning, I felt their power as oppressive and demanding. I had played fast and loose with my mother's wishes for years. But opposing my father, I realized, was an entirely different matter.

At last my sire replaced his pen on its stand, sanded what he had written, applied wax, and pressed the heavy seal of the ring of the Earl of Chase into the soft wax. Only then did he recognize my presence and motion me to a chair in front of his desk.

"Well, young lady, just what do you have to say for yourself?"

What had ever given me the idea that Papa's hazel eyes were mild and kindly? They were very like a falcon's. I turned my gaze to the right to avoid his glare, but was blinded by the morning sun streaming in from the French doors opening onto the garden. When I glanced back at Papa, I saw that he had placed my chair purposely so I would be hard put not to look directly at him as I spoke.

I straightened my shoulders and clenched my hands even more tightly in my lap.

"The nature of my . . . chat . . . with Lord Rochmont, was not what it appeared to be the moment you entered the library, Papa," I began.

"Correct me if I am suffering from some misapprehension, Constance, my dear. But what I witnessed was not what I would call a 'chat'. It was a much more direct form of communication. Did I, or did I not observe you in the arms of Lord Rochmont, being kissed by him?"

"Yes, Papa." I studied the flowers on my frock. "But . . ."

"Let me guess. Lord Rochmont rushed into the library, just moments before my arrival, tore a tome of edifying sermons from your trembling hands, and proceeded to indulge himself in the display which I witnessed."

"No, Papa, of course not." I summoned my courage and looked him in the eye. "But I assure you . . ."

"Come, come, Constance, I have no intention of accusing Lord Rochmont of ravishing you. Nor do I think for a second that anything of a truly scandalous nature went on in the Sandforth's library last night. That is just the point. You are no green girl. You have led numerous gentlemen a merry chase, and your poor Mama too, if the truth be known. Whether it was you or Rochmont who arrived at that confounded library first, there was simply no excuse for you to have remained there long enough to have sat down, much less had a 'chat' as you so coyly put it."

I could feel my face flush in embarrassment. But my father was just warming to his lecture.

"I have watched these four years and more while you have played the flibbertigibbet with one earnest young man after the other. And your dear adoring Mama! So worried about your future! So everlastingly hopeful! How many times has she asked me with a knowing look and breathless anticipation to 'hold myself available' for an important call from Lord Whatsits or Mr. Whatever? How many times have I consoled her when Lord Whatsits' or Mr. Whatever's betrothal to one of your dear friends was announced?

"I must confess that, initially, I was amused. After all, what doting father thinks any of his daughter's swains are really worthy of her? But your behavior has ceased to be entertaining. Before escorting you and your mama to London for one more season, I had promised myself I would not let your mother endure another such ordeal. She is not some weak-minded, hysterical creature. And for her to go into a decline, as she did last summer, was the result of years of repeated frustration. To see her in such a state is something I do not care to experience again! Indeed, I will not permit it!"

I was truly aghast. Not for one moment had I seen my game in such light. And I had not dreamed Papa had any knowledge of what I had been up to.

"I am so very, very sorry, Papa." I applied the small square of lace, which served as my handkerchief, to the corners of my eyes. "If you will just let Lord Rochmont know

that he is not obliged to wed me, I promise to make a fresh
start and find a husband that will please Mama."

"Bamwell, for example?"

Papa was not fighting fair. He accurately took my mute
look of horror as "Please, God, no!"

"Then Rochmont it will be."

It sounded like a sentence.

"But, Papa! I really do not know him at all! He is not even
English! Everyone knows that he pursues commerce! Mama
never would have considered him for me!"

"Enough, Constance!" Papa did not raise his voice, but it
was so cold, I shivered. "You know him sufficiently to have
spent an indeterminable time alone with him, leading to
what inevitably occurs in such situations. He may not *be* English, but he certainly *speaks* English as well as either you or
I. And you know very well that no one would dare snub him
for his commercial pursuits. Why, Grenaults held vast tracks
of land when most of our forbearers were trotting about in
animal skins. I do not doubt a Grenault was exercising *droit
de seigneur* when a Hautonne was acting as page to one of
William of Normandy's knights."

Good heavens! Papa *was* upset if he could be so indelicate
as to use a French phrase in my presence that Miss Holmes,
my governess, had never taught me.

"As for your mother's endless lists of eligibles, there was
not a man on one of them that could have kept up with your
pranks. I have no doubt, Rochmont can!"

I knew then for a certainty there was no hope my erst-
while doting father would spring the trap I had gotten myself
into. Some hint of my despair must have touched him. He
rose from his chair and came around the large desk, took my
hands, and pulled me to my feet.

"I blame myself as much as anyone for your unhappiness,
Constance, m'dear. You are your Mama's and my golden
girl. But, at three and twenty, you cannot expect to continue
to dance through life. Indeed, you will make yourself an object of ridicule if you choose to play the part of the perennial

toast. Your own Mama was already mother of three sons when she was your age.

"On the other hand, if you truly wish to follow in your Great Aunt Matilda's footsteps, I will not object. She has lived a satisfying life, full of intellectual inquiry and good works. But she never had your sparkle, your beauty, and your wonderful way of making life fun. Try as I might, I cannot picture you so removed from the whirl of society.

"So, it is my considered judgment that you need a husband. True, Rochmont is not pretending to be smitten with you. I doubt he ever will be blinded by your beauty, as have all too many unfortunate young men. But, I promise you that I know him to be honorable. And perhaps, in a way, you did choose each other. It is not just you who remained in the Sandforth's library to be discovered. He did too. And I have never known him to act without purpose."

Papa kissed my cheek, and opened the door, releasing me from what had felt like a particularly oppressive combination of court and confessional. But I felt no sense of escape as I made my way back to my room to consider what options might still be left to me. Not one immediately presented itself.

In such desperate circumstances, my mind naturally turned to my wardrobe. What does a lady wear to meet an unwelcome fate? I chose a gown of French blue (my private jest) silk of severest cut, with a bodice rising to my throat, featuring tiny tucks, and long, fitted sleeves. My only jewels were the very fine pearl necklace and earrings that Papa had presented me the evening of my come-out ball, which seemed to have occurred in a previous lifetime.

Having eaten a bite or two of the luncheon I had requested be sent to me on a tray, I repaired to the sitting room which afforded a view of the street. I was torn between hope and fear that Rochmont would fail to keep his appointment with Papa. If he failed to appear, would I then be free? Would Papa challenge him to a duel? Or would Papa see me betrothed to Bamwell? With that thought, I instantly regretted the few bites of lunch I had eaten.

Any idea that Rochmont might not appear was unfounded, for he proved to count promptness, if nothing else, as a virtue. At precisely twenty-eight minutes past two, a shiny black carriage drawn by matching sleek, highbred horses, pulled up to Hatton House. Although the carriage door displayed no crest, anyone would have instantly recognized the owner of such an equipage to be an important personage. Rochmont himself emerged from the carriage and made his way briskly up the front steps to the door, which Perkins, our ever-diligent butler, held open for him. No doubt, at the stroke of half past two, he was entering my father's study. At this time of day, there would be no sun pouring through the garden windows to discomfort him.

My summons would now come soon, I believed. I believed incorrectly. The dainty clock on the mantle ticked and ticked. I decided to pass the time with my long neglected stitchery. I knotted my embroidery thread, lost my thimble amongst the pillows, bit off the thread, dropped the needle, gave up any pretense of occupying myself with needlework, and began to pace. The clock chimed the quarter hour, then the hour. At last, Perkins appeared to lead me to the pretty little room adjacent to my father's study, where Rochmont awaited me.

He stood by the fireplace, very much as I had first seen him the night before, but sans cigar. He strode over to meet me, taking the cold hand that I offered, and with utmost correctness, kissed the air above it as he bowed. I heard the door click shut behind me. Perkins had his instructions.

"Lord Rochmont." I refused to let my voice shake, but I could hear the unaccustomed breathiness.

"Lady Constance."

As our eyes met, I realized I had been mistaken; his eyes were not black. Daylight revealed them to be very dark brown, the color of the coffee that Continental émigrés unaccountably preferred to tea. An unbidden image of the two of us at the breakfast table flashed before me, Rochmont drinking his bitter brew, I sipping delicately at my favorite China blend. I could feel myself flush.

I was quickly seated on a delicate "lady's chair". The French lord knelt before me asking me "to make him the most fortunate of men" by consenting to become his bride. To which I responded dryly, "it seems that I shall."

If I meant to offend him by my less than enthusiastic acceptance, I was disappointed. As he stood, I detected a half smile on his harsh face, and perhaps a hint of appreciation for my honesty. He then took my left hand, and, on the third finger, placed upon it what can only be described as the most extraordinary diamond ring I had ever seen. It was a ring that would impress a Maharani. Perhaps it had. I did not care to ask. I suspected I would need to develop new strength in order to lift my left hand under my own power.

Rochmont shrugged, the only Gallicism I had yet to detect in his demeanor.

"A sapphire might have been more expected for a blue-eyed blonde, but I found I could not resist a diamond of the first water for a lady who is, indeed, a diamond of the first water."

I lost all coherent thought as I felt the same confusion I had experienced in this man's presence the previous evening. If he noticed anything amiss, he did not show it, but took the larger "gentleman's chair" across from where I sat.

"Believe me, Lady Constance, I do appreciate the awkwardness of the situation in which we find ourselves," he began in those soothing tones that had quite mesmerized me the night before. I determined to keep my wits about me as he continued.

"I do understand that just yesterday you had no notion that today you would be engaged to a man whom you had not yet met, and would not have chosen for your husband had you chanced to have met him. But I am persuaded, with the passage of time, you will find yourself more reconciled to this unexpected turn of fate than you might presently think possible."

An infinitesimal lift of an eyebrow punctuated this opinion.

"Perhaps there are some rather mundane matters which, if settled, would, if not render you comfortable, at least might diminish your discomfort. For example, the basic question of my name. It is true, although the English persist in addressing me as "my lord", and "Rochmont", I have never styled myself so. My father was a devoted follower of the most egalitarian ideals of the Revolution, and happily renounced his title and all the trappings of the aristocracy, much to my mother's dismay and disapproval. Well before his encounter with the guillotine, he had asked to be called 'Citoyen Grenault'.

"When I began to make my own way in the world as a young lad, it did not seem likely that the ship's captain who took me on as a cabin boy would be impressed by my calling myself The Marquis de Rochmont and insisting upon being addressed as 'my lord'. Indeed, I rapidly became known as 'Greeno" to the entire crew.

"But, of course, times have changed dramatically since then, including King Louis' restoration of titles. So, if you prefer, I shall resume the title and you will be the Marquise de Rochmont after we wed. Quite candidly, my dear Lady Constance, as far as I am concerned, you may call yourself whatever pleases you. If you wish to continue to be addressed as 'Lady Constance', such a thing is not without precedent for the daughter of an earl. Or, as I have mentioned, if you wish to be called 'Lady Rochmont', I will change my cards and signet ring." I glanced at the large onyx he wore, and discerned the initials 'BdG' elaborately scrolled on it.

He noticed my glance and smiled briefly. "Perhaps my late, radical father did not forsake all the trappings of his birth. After his death, his ring with the Rochmont crest was sent anonymously to my mother here in England. She gave it to me, charging me with the need to avenge my father—a charge I put away with the ring. It would be a simple matter to change rings. It is a ruby though," he shuddered. "Whatever would Brummel think?

"Or," he continued, "you could be 'Madame Blaise de Grenault', or Mrs. Blaise de Grenault', or 'Connie Greeno'." He favored me with a brilliant smile. "And to think you supposed you had run out of choices!"

Maybe it was because he had given voice to exactly what I was supposing—that I had run out of choices—I felt most untimely and unwelcome tears fill my eyes. As I endeavored to blink them away, he pressed a soft man-sized handkerchief into my hand. And I had not even returned the one he had lent me the previous evening.

"Perhaps I have misjudged the situation." His voice sounded truly kind. "Are your affections engaged? Did I incorrectly assume your detachment?"

I shook my head, dabbing my cheeks gently, so as not to smear the tiny bit of rouge I had been forced to use in order to appear my natural self.

"That is just the problem!" I blurted out, and regretted it instantly. Why did my common sense evaporate when I was in this man's company?

"Ah, I begin to see the way of things with the lovely Lady Constance."

I hoped to heaven Lord Rochmont's vision was not as acute as he apparently thought it was, that he did not perceive my most treasured dream was for a husband who adored me, who adored me sufficiently that he would indulge my whims and make *my* happiness his concern as much as it was my own. I suspected such a notion would provide Lord Rochmont with no end of amusement.

"Of course, you wish to marry for love! Quite understandable. The idea of a love match is all the rage these days. That explains all the elusive maneuvers over the past years."

He sounded as if he had solved a rather simple puzzle.

"And not unreasonably, you now view me as a potentially permanent impediment to achieving your goal. A most unsympathetic role to find oneself playing, I must say."

Although Rochmont did not appear stricken by this state of affairs, I began offering him my apologies.

"It is nothing personal, my lord," I assured him earnestly. "It is just that I had always hoped . . . perhaps even assumed . . . I just expected mine would be, as you said, a *love match*." I finished in hurried embarrassment.

Better he think I was a hopeless romantic than to understand that what I really wanted was blind devotion in a husband. I suspected that, while he might believe the desire for a love match might be unrealistically romantic, he would respect such a goal. But Lord Rochmont was forcing me, for the first time, to consider my requirements in a husband from a potential husband's point of view. I feared giving voice to my longing for adoration might somehow lessen me in this inconveniently perceptive gentleman's eyes.

If Lord Rochmont, or Mr. de Grenault, or whatever I decided to call him, caught my embarrassment, he showed no indication. Instead, he seemed to consider the substance of my mortifyingly emotional outpouring as a problem to be solved.

"Now, let me see," his reasoned tones were beginning to send off alarms in the recesses of my brain, the tiny part of that organ apparently still functioning.

"One may assume that your search for this fortunate gentleman whose ardor you could reciprocate has remained unsuccessful for more than four years."

I nodded in agreement, wishing to impress him with my cool rationality.

"True," I affirmed.

He continued, fingers steepled in an attitude of considered thought, which gave me an excellent opportunity to study his onyx ring. It suited him so well it seemed a pity that he would consider replacing it with a garish ruby.

"Now, I know of no learned opinions about the average length of search for true love."

The onyx, rimmed in gold was without blemish. Obviously Rochmont did not use this ring for sealing letters.

"But it seems to me that more than four years of sustained devotion to such a quest is a considerable portion of one's life. Religious pilgrimages do not usually consume as much time, I am quite certain."

Why had I let my thoughts wander? I felt the necessity to nod again in agreement. Who was I to argue about the length of religious pilgrimages? And I was feeling every one of those four years of what Lord Rochmont called my search for true love.

"Furthermore, it is an observable phenomenon, that not all humans are fortunate enough to ever experience the enchantment of being prized as much—or even more—than they prize their loved one. Indeed, most must accept and make do with the respect, good will, and loyalty of their mates. In fact, it has been my observation that such marriages are generally happier long term than those based on the vagaries of feelings. It seems to me that emotions are notoriously changeable."

This time, I hesitated a moment before nodding. Rochmont's discourse had taken a turn which made me vaguely uncomfortable.

"So, what I am suggesting is this."

Now his words, not his ring, had my full attention.

"If between now, and say, six months' time, you find the love of your life, I will release you from our engagement so you may wed the gentleman you love. If, on the other hand, the love of your life has not appeared, we will be married, and I shall endeavor to make you as happy as it is possible for you to be, under such constrained circumstances."

He sat calmly awaiting my answer. I should have known his philosophical speculation was directed toward a purpose. And, in all candor, I had to admit what he said was perfectly reasonable, if totally lacking in romantic sentiment.

"A year," the breathiness was back in my voice. I swallowed and said, more distinctly, "I would like another year, and if I am not in love with another who also loves me, I will marry you."

He gave me his half smile, and I suspected he had guessed exactly where our bargaining would lead.

"Now, I imagine we should share the happy news of our

engagement with your parents. I am quite certain our private understanding would be of no interest to them."

For once I was in complete agreement with Blaise de Grenault, Lord Rochmont.

Chapter Three

Initially, being engaged seemed to be a great deal less stressful than becoming engaged. While waiting for Papa and Mama to join us in a celebratory glass of champagne, my newly betrothed suggested that I call him "Blaise".

"I believe I prefer to call you 'Rochmont' ".

I realized I would have to guard against slipping into an easy familiarity that would make my extrication from our betrothal even more problematic than I already knew it would be. It was tempting to call such a challenging man by his given name, but I resisted.

"But do feel free to call me Constance."

Considering the names my three elder brothers had called me over the years, Constance was the height of formality.

Mama made her appearance on Papa's arm. She had apparently experienced a miraculous recovery from her headache. In times of crisis, Mama resorts to her jewel box. For this occasion, she had draped herself in the Chase emeralds. She paused at the threshold, beaming and dabbing at her eyes with a lace handkerchief before offering her very best wishes and congratulations.

"Constance dearest," she managed in a trembling voice. "My own darling baby! It scarcely seems possible that you are going to be leaving your dear Papa and me."

That was true. She had despaired of ever marrying me off.

She then turned to Rochmont, who accepted her embrace with great equanimity.

"Welcome, welcome to our family, Lord Rochmont. I can only think of your dear, courageous mama. Poor, darling Clothilde! How tragic that she cannot be with us today! But how very happy she is, looking down on us from her heavenly home."

Again, Mama applied lace to eye. It was a surprise to me, and I believe also to Papa and Lord Rochmont, that Mama had ever known, much less remembered, the name of the late Marquise de Rochmont, who, during her brief years in exile rarely left the tight circle of French émigrés who mistakenly expected Louis XVI to mount a successful counter-revolution rather than the scaffold.

We managed to make and receive the usual toasts: to the happy couple—my fiancé and I put on our best social smiles. To the parents of the bride—Mama and Papa's beaming seemed genuine. To the blessed memory of the prospective bridegroom's parents. Mama's handkerchief made another appearance.

As my newly betrothed prepared to depart, Papa handed a note to Perkins, asking that it be delivered to the offices of *The Gazette*. No doubt it was the engagement announcement. It looked very much like what I had seen him writing before our morning chat. It dawned on me that my fate had been sealed—even before my morning ordeal with Papa.

To say that Daisy was happy when she learned of my engagement is to indulge in profound understatement. She had received the "happy news" of my interview with Rochmont from the highly reliable servants' network as she was laundering the crumpled handkerchief I had left in my reticule the previous evening.

"And there I were, my lady, doing up your things, and I were studying that hannerchief, like. I knowed right off it were a gennelman's, so large it were and all, and so spanking white, it like to have blinded me. But them letters was that hard to make out, all swirlly and all. They looked like a great 'B' and a little 'd' and a great 'G', and I were just saying to myself, I were, 'he must be some really grand noble, he must, to have somethin' like that on his hannerchief.' No wonder you wasn't quite yourself, my lady. You must have been that thrilled to be contemplatin' matrimony and all."

I managed a wan smile, which I hoped Daisy would interpret as an expression of joy too deep for words.

The *ton's* reaction to the announcement of the intended marriage of Lady Constance Agatha Mary Hatton to Blaise Dominic Louis de Grenault, Marquis de Rochmont was gratifying, if one chose to believe it was based on peoples' eagerness to express wishes for the couple's future happiness; insulting, if one thought it reflected amazement that the prospective bride had finally found a candidate for the role of prospective bridegroom.

On the day the announcement appeared in *The Gazette,* visitors arrived as soon as did visiting hours, scores of visitors. Mama had worked diligently for this day, and although her labors had not contributed directly to its arrival, she did not let that technicality deter her from presenting a face of knowing delight. If her social rivals hoped to detect a hint of discomposure over Rochmont's foreign origins, his reputation as a ladies' man, or the suddenness of the engagement, they were soon disappointed.

Mama sprinkled her conversation with her best schoolroom French. "*Je suis enchantee, mes cheres amies! Quel bonheur, je vous assure!*" How could one make snide remarks about a Frenchman when one's hostess was attempting to speak the French language?

"My own dearest Great Aunt Honoria for whom I was named, you know, my dear Louisa, always counseled that men who take their time in settling on their chosen lady, make the most devoted of husbands," Mama told Louisa Fortesque, a rigid upholder of morals and propriety, not only for her brow-beaten family, but also the entire top ten thousand.

And when Maria Canfield-Gould inquired archly if, perhaps Rochmont's interest in Lady Constance had not come as something of a surprise, Mama owned with a knowing look and confiding tone that "Chase and I had observed 'for some time now' a discreet, but decidedly flattering preference Rochmont was showing our dear Constance."

It was a bold-faced lie, of course. But Mama's performance was so convincing, I found myself trying to recall any instance when Rochmont had so much as glanced my way before our fateful encounter in the Sandforth's library. I could remember no such instance.

Then, there was the matter of the engagement ring. Lady Redell, sister in spite to Maria Canfield-Gould, demanded loudly, "Has anyone ever seen a ring of such size presented by a *gentleman* to a *lady*?"

But Mama was prepared.

"Is it not true, my dear Lady Redell," she replied mistily. "How often can one find a gentleman with the means to express so fully the depth of his regard for his intended? Constance is the most fortunate of creatures, I declare!"

Visitors were obliged to share Mama's happiness or keep their reservations to themselves.

That evening, Rochmont had invited me, along with Mama and Papa, to share his box at the opera. It was to be our first public appearance together as an engaged couple. I wanted to look my best, not to impress my new fiancé, but for pride's sake. Rochmont was known as a connoisseur of women, and I did not want people to compare me unfavorably with the numerous beauties in whose company he had been seen.

I knew I could count on Daisy, if she could but channel her enthusiasm for my engagement into assisting my toilette. After much debate, we settled on a gown of *eau de Nile* silk chiffon, which floated about my person in soft whispers. My jewels were earrings and necklace of particularly fine, clear aquamarines. In my hair, rather than the usual tiara, I wore gardenias. I do not think I imagined the flicker of appreciation in Rochmont's eyes as he watched me descend the staircase to the foyer where he waited.

When our little party entered the box, a hush fell over the entire audience. Perhaps people were as shocked as I over my betrothal and the indisputable evidence that Rochmont and I, as unlikely a couple as could be imagined, really were engaged to be married.

Then, the volume of chatter arose to a deafening level, with Rochmont and me, no doubt, the topic of conversation. I glanced at Mama, who glowed in supreme triumph. She was wearing magenta satin, accessorized with the Chase diamonds, complete with tiara. She was nodding and smiling to those who turned our way, much I fancy as Juno might have, if all her divine children had ever decided simultaneously to do her bidding.

I turned to Rochmont and found him looking at me with a raised eyebrow and a slight smile. I could feel a responding flush beginning at my décolletage and climbing rapidly to my face. When the houselights dimmed and the curtain rose, I was so relieved, I focused intently on the performance— something I had never done before in my years of attending the opera.

At first this course of action seemed the safest. If I looked at the audience, I met undisguised stares. If I looked at the man beside me, I found it difficult to remember to breathe. So I concentrated on the story of poor Orfeo and Euridice. The pathos of their love and the delicacy of the music were profoundly touching. I was inexorably drawn into the ancient story about just the sort of devotion I had longed to inspire in the gentleman I would marry.

Attending closely to the performance had been a safe refuge initially, but as Orfeo searched for his beloved in the underworld and attempted to lead her to safety without gazing on her, I could scarcely hold back tears. Then, when he lost her again, I lost what fragile control I had maintained and began to cry in earnest. My delicate linen square was already sodden from dabbing at my eyes discreetly from time to time during the performance. I knew Mama, who was seated to my right, would be of no help.

According to Mama, the proper use of tears is an art. Spontaneous crying is to be avoided at all costs. Tears are to lend starry glitter to one's eyes, draw attention to one's exquisite sensibilities, or, in extreme situations, remind a gentleman that he is not fully appreciating one's sacrifices. But tears are never to actually fall. Mama finds the thought of unplanned crying to be decidedly off-putting. And Mama makes it a rule to ignore whatever she finds off-putting.

Not only was I crying, with real tears coursing down my cheeks, I feared that I might soon sob audibly. Just as I began to tremble in an effort to regain some control, Rochmont came to my rescue, tucking another of his handkerchiefs into my right hand and taking my left hand in his, transmitting comfort and strength. After one tiny hiccup, which he pretended not to notice, I was able to recapture my composure.

As the opera ended, Rochmont reached over and nudged back a gardenia, which had come loose from my coiffure. He drew a finger down the side of my cheek and held my chin, apparently assessing the damages inflicted by my emotional display.

"I believe you will do," he pronounced.

Did he notice that I failed to breathe as I gazed into his dark, opaque eyes, trying to discover if there was a meaning deeper in his words than the obvious? But he betrayed nothing as he assisted me with my cloak and we departed.

Our engagement was a great deal less troublesome for me when he was out of sight.

When Daisy made her loquacious appearance the following morning, neither my forthcoming marriage nor the laundering of linen squares embroidered "BdG" was her topic of conversation.

"It's a glorious morning, my lady! Glorious and . . . my lady, how wonnerful his honourable has been spared to us, come home safe and whole he is, thank the Dear Lord above."

She clasped her hands in prayerful attitude and turned her face heavenward.

In her enthusiasm, she had deposited my teacup on the table by the door, so I struggled to decipher her message without the aid of so much as a sip of tea.

"Who . . . ?" I began.

But Daisy was too full of her news to hear.

"Course I din't speak to him personal, like. But Ruthie and me peeked over the banister while he was talkin' to Perkins. Breaks your heart it does—Ruthie agreed—to think of such a fine gennelman in war's danger."

A tear trembled on Daisy's eyelash.

"The war's been over for close to a year now, Daisy. And I would like my tea before it cools, or my tranquility will be in danger."

Daisy apologized profusely while correcting her error.

"But I thought you would be full of joy, my lady, at his return to the bosom of his loved ones."

The tea must have helped my brain. For the identity of the unnamed "his honourable" became clear. Daisy was rhapsodizing about the return of my brother, Captain, the Honourable John William Hatton. I presume that for Daisy, Jack's "loved ones" referred to his family, although truth be told, other bosoms of other loved ones would soon be enjoying reunion with him too.

It was inevitable that my naïve, country-bred maid would be enthralled by the charms of Darling Jack. He had been the scourge of female hearts and hopes since he was breeched. It was true that he had seen war in the Peninsula, but he had most recently been with the occupying armies in Paris. Why he had quit that city for London at this particular time I could only guess. The involvement of some female would be a safe wager.

Not that I lack affection for Jack, who, being seven years

my senior, is closest to me in age of my three brothers. I do love him. But in my state of mind on that particular morning, I was challenged to summon the energy needed to deal with what can only be described as a force of nature, a force who was now decamped in the household.

In spite of my lack of enthusiasm for being awakened by Daisy's bright chatter, I had reason to thank her for a timely warning when, upon opening the door to the breakfast room, I was grabbed at the waist, kissed repeatedly, twirled and hoisted as if I were a ballet dancer.

"Connie, Connie, beautiful as ever, didn't I tell you, Rick, lad?"

Over Jack's shoulder I glimpsed from time to time a dark-haired gentleman who had risen when I entered the room.

When I was at last set upon my feet and the spinning of my head ceased sufficiently for me to focus, I gazed up into a face that after a period of separation always struck me with its unique appeal. Jack was square-jawed, and the faint lines on his face that were the result of his years of exposure to the Spanish sun had endowed him with the appearance of character. His nose was straight like Mama's. His hair was the same gold as my own, but it was just slightly wavy rather than curly. A handsome man by any standard. But what gave him unfair advantage was a pair of the most deceptively guileless blue eyes framed in thick, curling lashes. The overall effect, in spite of his broad shoulders and more than six feet of height, convinced unwary females that Jack was in need of coddling and understanding. Unfortunately, coddling and understanding were what females who lost their hearts to Jack needed.

"Let me see you, Connie."

He took my hands and stepped back to study me, but my ring caught his attention. His astonishment was gratifying if less than flattering. His astonishment grew when he learned to whom I was betrothed.

"You minx! How did you ever manage to snare such a wily one?" was all he could manage in the way of best wishes.

His surprise was genuine, for I had to prompt him to re-member to introduce me to his friend.

Major Cedric Howells pronounced himself delighted to make my acquaintance. He was slightly shorter and more squarely built than Jack. His gray eyes and straight brows under straight brown hair gave him an air of quiet serious-ness. Jack explained that Major Howells' nabob uncle had recently passed to his eternal reward, leaving his temporal reward to "Rick", his only nephew.

Since Paris had become "deuced dull", Jack had volun-teered to accompany Major Howells to London while the major's financial matters were put in order. They both in-tended to sell their commissions, and Jack had nominated himself sponsor of Major Howells' first foray into London society. They bid me farewell, off to consult Weston for civilian wardrobes.

If Major Howells wished to be tutored in ways to relieve his sobriety and spend his fortune, my brother Jack was the man for the task.

As happy as I was at Jack's departure and the postpone-ment of the prospect of answering his questions about how I had "managed to snare such a wily one", solitude was not my best friend that morning. I had not slept well the night before. My rest had been disturbed by a recurring dream, a dream that placed me in the role of Euridice, the tragic hero-ine of last evening's opera. But unlike the opera, the under-world of my dream was subtly transformed into London society. Wandering this "underworld", I repeatedly found myself in some scrape or embarrassment. My sandal lacing came untied during a quadrille. I spilled champagne on my gown. I was caught in a downpour in an open carriage. Each time, I was rescued, and when I turned in gratitude to my rescuer, I looked into the opaque gaze of Rochmont.

I had no need to consult an expert in esoteric matters for insight into this dream. Apparently some primitive, naïve portion of my psyche perceived the Marquis de Rochmont as a knight in shining armor who had rescued me from the rigors of endless London seasons. While it was true that our betrothal had freed me from the tiresome game I had played with Mama and my suitors, common sense told me that attaching any tender feelings to Rochmont would be a serious blunder, if I wished to extract myself from our ridiculous engagement and replace him with a less inscrutable and more pliable fiancé.

Fully awake and away from him, I could remember he was a stranger, a man of infinite calculation and extensive experience with the fair sex. In order to retain some semblance of dignity for the duration of our engagement, it was necessary that I keep my wits about me. But in Rochmont's presence, my wits too often deserted me. Now, he was troubling my rest. How could I extricate myself from this situation without a decent night's sleep?

My thoughts turned to the past four seasons and I reviewed my suitors with considerable fondness. Why had I not appreciated their open devotion? What had been so irritating about predictable admiration? How had I managed to whistle down the wind so many opportunities to establish my own home with someone who did not threaten my ability to act and think rationally? Someone, for example, such as Major Howells . . . The more I thought about the good major, the more appealing he became. His clear gray eyes, his solid, almost stocky appearance, his age—which I guessed to be closer to forty than to thirty—spoke of reliability and security. Surely he could be led to see that if he truly loved a lady, it would be natural to indulge her every whim: that *his* perfect happiness would lie in his *beloved's* perfect happiness. The more I considered Major Howells, the more likely a prospect he seemed to be the ideal replacement for Lord Rochmont.

How difficult could it be to engage his interest? Even if he did not remain a guest at Hatton House for the duration of the season, it was clear from what Jack had said that he planned to remain in London. And as Jack's friend, he would be thrown into my company repeatedly. True, I had never before planned to attach a particular gentleman. But, since I had attracted more than my share without trying, I was certain of my success, if for once, I actually set my mind to the project.

Rochmont's face sprang to mind, unbidden and unwelcome. How would I convince my fiancé I loved Major Howells? After all, the bargain I had struck with Rochmont required that I find a love match. Perhaps I would be inspired when Major Howells declared himself. True, previous declarations had never inspired me to love. But this time I would be grateful, I was certain. And gratitude is very loving in its own way, I assured myself.

Not wishing to examine the implications of my thoughts too closely, I decided to pay a visit to Hookam's Circulating Library. A quantity of reading material would serve as a welcome diversion.

With Daisy in tow, I walked the short distance to that unexceptionable establishment, and, to my dismay, encountered Mrs. Harold Fortesque, or, as Mama named her between clenched teeth, "Dear Louisa".

With Mrs. Fortesque was a young lady who on first sight had little to recommend her. Her clothing could most charitably be described as nondescript. Her hair was pulled back severely from her face, and was all but hidden by a particularly undistinguished bonnet. Her figure, which would have been stunning on someone of reasonable height, in one so short, would forever compromise even the most skilled dressmaker's attempts at elegance. But anyone about to dismiss her as a hopeless nonentity failed to appreciate an extraordinary pair of golden-green eyes, flawless, milky white complexion, and a perfect oval face.

"Lady Constance, permit me to present my niece, Miss Drusilla Fortesque," Mrs. Fortesque was saying. "She is the daughter of the son of my late husband's unfortunate brother, Chester."

Miss Fortesque was a lady of admirable self-control, for she betrayed no reaction to this astounding introduction and comported herself as a model of proper conduct in her acknowledgment of her aunt's introduction.

But "Dear Louisa" had not finished her task of identifying the extent of Miss Fortesque's indebtedness to her. She announced in a voice carrying to the farthest corners of the library that her poor niece had been languishing in Bath for the past three years, acting as companion to "some aging connection" of her mother's family. A wave of her hand punctuated just how ordinary Miss Fortesque's mother's family was.

"And so, when I heard of the poor girl's plight, I determined to give her a treat and bring her to London for the season."

Mrs. Fortesque did not mention that another distant relation, a shy young miss, had served as her companion during the previous season. That young lady attracted the notice of a captain recently retired from His Majesty's Navy. The captain's pockets were quite plump with prize money, and even though his family origins had been pronounced without merit by Mrs. Fortesque, the shy young miss had accepted his suit, leaving Dear Louisa without an attendant.

For Mrs. Fortesque believed it was the calling of indigent relatives to dance attention upon her, to read to her all of the announcements and *on dits* in *The Gazette,* and nod in agreement with her when she delivered her protracted commentaries on the shortcomings of family and acquaintances. So Miss Drusilla Fortesque had been summoned from Bath to wait on her tyrannical great aunt. What a "treat"! I hoped the pity I felt didn't show on my face.

At that moment, Mrs. Percival Canfield-Gould made her entrance, and Louisa Fortesque hastened to rid herself of unwanted company so she could have an uninterrupted exchange with her fellow gossip. Miss Fortesque was dispatched to find the Reverend Mr. Clegbourne's *Edifying Sermons for Ladies.* Leaving Daisy to gape out the front window at the passing scene, I accompanied Miss Fortesque on her errand.

She proceeded directly to the section devoted to theology and sermons, pulled down a slim volume, and asked where novels and poetry could be found.

I was astonished.

"You must read prodigiously fast, to find Mr. Clegbourne's sermons so instantaneously," I allowed.

I was surprised by her low gurgle of laughter.

"Whyever would I bother to read the titles? Sermons are much alike, are they not? And I am certain that Great Aunt Louisa would profit equally from any she might read—or have me read to her, more likely."

Her contralto tones lent an air of conspiracy to her words. Having dispatched both errand and aunt, she enquired about more important concerns.

"Do you think they have a copy of *The Corsair*? It is so embarrassing to admit I have not yet read it. And a swashbuckling brigand sounds appealing."

I should not have been surprised that such a drab looking creature harbored such decidedly undrab ideas. I knew I was one of very few ladies who did not, in their secret hearts, nurture a passion for the scandalous Lord Byron. Even so, I felt it was only fair to introduce some realism, in case Miss Fortesque had permitted herself the hope her London season would be marked by a dalliance with the notorious peer.

"It is, indeed, a stirring epic," I allowed, "and I am certain we can find it here for you. But, if what is said is true, and Lord Byron modeled the hero of *The Corsair* on himself, he shares too many of that pirate's character flaws. I fear, Miss Fortesque, that he is no longer being received. In fact, there is a strong possibility he will have to go into exile, at least until the most recent scandal surrounding him is forgotten."

I prayed Miss Fortesque would forbear asking the nature of the most recent scandal. I pride myself on a degree of sophistication, but even sophistication has its limits.

Once again, I was surprised by my companion. She laughed her soft, low laugh.

"Never fear, my dear Lady Constance. I am not an impressionable female who believes all a reprobate like Lord Byron needs is the love of a good lady. Has not Lady Byron proved that to be a misapprehension? Poor thing! Indeed," she whispered to me, "do not breathe a word of it to a soul, that I infinitely prefer novels such as *First Impressions* to the poetry of Lord Byron. But it is ever so much more amusing to affect devotion to the Scandalous Lord!"

I suspected Louisa Fortesque was going to have a more eventful season than she had anticipated.

Having made my own selections, and bidding Mrs. and Miss Fortesque farewell, I went to retrieve Daisy for the walk home. But I discovered her attention had been captured by a scene just across the street from Hookam's.

There, sparkling in the morning light was Lady Antony Compton, nee Miss Madeleine Sedgewick, the toast of the season of 1811, the year prior to the year of my debut.

Some said I owed my own success to the fact that the possibilities of brunette loveliness had been exhausted by the perfection of Miss Sedgewick, making a blonde inevitable the following year. Certainly, Lady Antony's beauty would be difficult to exaggerate.

She had been absent from London for almost three years, but, if anything, she was more stunning than ever. Heated arguments had arisen over which of her features most closely represented perfection. Was it her soft pale complexion that resembled the petal of a dewy, white rose? Was it her cherry-red lips, shaped in a perfect bow that lifted gently at its corners? Was it the porcelain column of her neck? Or the cloud of black curls? Each feature had its partisans, but it was a pair of deep pansy-blue eyes under perfectly arched brows, most agreed, that drew and held one when encountering Lady Antony. Her innate sense of what was most becoming to her had in no way diminished. An ensemble of a blue almost shading into lavender highlighted her ethereal beauty that spring morning.

Her return would undoubtedly be an important event. Arriving in London six years earlier with no dowry to speak of, her beauty alone had motivated any number of gentlemen to offer for her. But from all her suitors, she had chosen the profligate second son of the Duke of Addington, Lord Antony Compton, to be her husband. It had been said that if any lady could keep him by her side, the beauteous Madeleine could.

She had presented Lord Antony with a son and they had been the darlings of society. But Lord Antony met his end in a tragic riding accident that had cost his horse's life too.

Lady Antony had remained in seclusion for her full year of mourning. When that period had been extended, some wondered if Lady Antony ever would return to society. Now, the answer to that question was apparent. She was back, glorious as ever. But this time she had her bride settlement intact. She could remarry if she chose. Or, she might decide to engage in a discreet affair. She was just the sort of widow some sophisticated gentlemen preferred. She was engaged in rapt conversation with just such a gentleman: my fiancé, Lord Rochmont.

Chapter Four

Upon returning home, I settled down to read one of the
novels I had brought from Hookam's. It concerned a normally
dutiful and obedient daughter who had been locked in her
room by her wicked parents. They were determined to marry
her off to a debauched roué in order to recover their fortunes.
Our heroine was surviving on bread and water alone, formu-
lating a clever escape, despite her growing physical weakness.
A very affecting story, which so absorbed me, I was startled to
find that Daisy had entered the room, a missive in her hand.

"Pardon me, my lady, but Lord Rochmont has writ you a
note, and Monsewer Armand insists that it be answered
without delay!"

Daisy's freckled face was flushed and her breath was
coming in little gasps. She held the note tightly to her chest.

Whatever had "Monsewer Armand" said or done to get
Daisy into such a state, I wondered? When Daisy recovered
sufficiently to relinquish the note, I read:

Dear Constance,
I thought, perhaps, you might enjoy a turn in the
park this afternoon?

Blaise

I wrote a quick note of acceptance and gave it to Daisy to
convey to Rochmont's man. As she was leaving, she quickly

glanced in a looking glass, surreptitiously straightening her fichu and checking the set of her cap.

I indulged myself in a tiny moan. As if I did not have enough concerns for myself, thanks to my French fiancé! Now he had introduced another complicating factor into my life with his, no doubt, ingratiating and flirtatious servant! How could a simple country girl like Daisy possibly protect herself against the practiced wiles of a hardened seducer? I could easily picture M. Armand's type: a preening coxcomb with oiled hair, waxed mustache, reeking of patchouli. I would need to have a serious discussion with his master.

I would also need to give careful thought to my ensemble for the proposed outing. I settled on a creamy yellow muslin embroidered in lilies of the valley. My bonnet was of natural straw trimmed with wide cream satin ribbons, a bunch of silk lilies of the valley on the left side. When Rochmont greeted me, he murmured "Primavera", as he bent to kiss the air over my gloved hand. I chose to take this as a sign of approval.

His phaeton and pair were all of the same shade of grey, and he handled them with the ease that he apparently handled everything he did. When we had gained the park, I decided it was time to broach the subject of his servant's behavior toward Daisy.

"There is a matter which concerns me, that I wish to discuss with you," I began.

I realized the delicacy of the situation, and only my loyalty to and concern for Daisy prevailed upon me to pursue it with Rochmont, who might not appreciate its seriousness.

He gave me a thoughtful look.

"I believe I shall pull over here out of the way of other carriages so I can give the matter my undivided attention."

He matched action to words, making me feel slightly foolish. I was not at all comfortable having his undivided attention for this or any other matter, but it seemed I would have it. Rochmont turned to me, his face composed in sympathetic helpfulness.

"It is about my maid, Daisy," I began awkwardly.

For a moment, his expression went blank, almost confused, but he resumed his look of sympathetic helpfulness, and nodded encouragingly. I continued gamely.

"You see, Rochmont, Daisy is the greenest and most naïve and . . . romantical of country girls. This is her very first trip to London. And she is simply too vulnerable to charming lady's men. I am certain that your man . . . Armand, is his name? I am certain that he means no harm or insult. But I fear Daisy is in danger of succumbing to his wiles, and she really should not be left to the mercies of a practiced flirt . . . or worse."

Rochmont blinked twice and studied a nearby tree branch for a moment.

"You are certain that Armand is the object of your maid's infatuation?"

I affirmed that I was.

"Then, by all means, I shall speak to him. We cannot risk worry lines on such a beautiful face now, can we."

He laid a hand against the side of my cheek. His hand smelled faintly of leather and tobacco, an aroma I discovered to be very pleasant indeed. His thumb stroked lazily across my lips, and I found myself leaning ever so slightly toward him. I was beginning to find it difficult to breathe as his intention of kissing me became apparent. This, I knew, would be no brief brush of the lips.

"Monsieur le Marquis! Rochmont! Blaise! Cheri!"

A feminine voice shattered the moment. Rochmont let out a low growl. I felt very much the way one does when awakened from a particularly delightful dream, disoriented and disappointed.

Approaching us in a handsome barouche was a remarkable vision. Her elaborate bonnet did nothing to hide her hair—a fiery shade of orange-red—that I suspected owed more to her hairdresser's art than to her antecedents. Her eyes, under heavy lids, were the color of warm caramel. Her full mouth was punctuated just below the right corner with a beauty mark. It made one understand the rage for patches in Grandmama's day. It also made one wonder why they had ever gone out of fashion.

This extraordinary creature was dressed in a coppery orange gown that set off her hair, as did the neckline, an ample bosom. Next to her sat a hatchet-faced female, designed, no doubt, to lend the vision respectability, if, indeed, anything could.

The flame-haired beauty paid no notice of me, but tilted her head coquettishly and addressed Rochmont in rapid French. Miss Holmes' *vocabulaire* and *grammaire* drills were sufficient for me to understand that seeing darling Blaise again was quite the happiest of events she could possibly imagine. That Paris, as any city without his presence, had become quite insupportable. That she had been completely disconsolate in her longing to see his dear face again. That she was confident the resumption of their friendship would render them both most ecstatic.

Rochmont's "dear" face remained impassive throughout this outpouring. When there was a pause, he turned to me and said, "Constance, my dear, let me present to you Lady Edmund Norham. Lady Norham, my betrothed, Lady Constance Hatton."

If he had calculated that a dose of punctilious good manners would deter Lady Norham, he was much mistaken.

She subjected me to a sweeping, assessing glance, much as a knowledgeable judge of horseflesh would look at a particularly showy, but totally untried filly. Heavy lids shaded her eyes for a moment, and her mouth formed a tiny moue.

"Cette une enfante jolie, Blaise, cheri, mais . . . pourquoi?"

She smiled up at my fiancé, as if to say his lapse of judgment in my case was amusing, but certainly could not be taken seriously in the sophisticated world to which they both belonged.

"Lady Norham wishes to compliment you on your fresh, unspoiled beauty, Constance, my dear. It has been an age since she has seen its match."

I received another insight into Rochmont's success in international commerce. If a bit of communication did not appeal to him or suit his purposes, he fabricated one that would.

Anger flashed briefly in Lady Norham's eyes, but then a look of surprised recognition took its place. I was favored with a brilliant smile that almost made me doubt what I had been hearing and seeing just moments before.

"Lady Constance Hatton!" She exclaimed. "But you must be the sister of the brave and so charming Captain Jack . . . or is it John Hatton?"

It seemed that Lady Norham had an easy command of the English language when she chose to use it.

I was suddenly on very familiar ground. Over the years, how many female faces had brightened when they learned that I was Darling Jack Hatton's sister? How many "dear friends" had I acquired until they discovered that I could do nothing to influence my darling brother's choice of female favorites? I would not care to count them all. But I did wonder if Lady Norham had played some role in Jack's abrupt departure from Paris.

By this time, other carriages were approaching, and with an effusive expression of delight in making my acquaintance and a melting look at Rochmont, Lady Norham bid us *adieu*. She left me with a troubling assortment of suspicions and uncertainties, which I endeavored to forget in the friendly chatter that ensued as the *ton* engaged in seeing and being seen at that fashionable hour. My spirits had almost been restored, when a lady mounted on a pretty bay mare paused by the phaeton.

"Lord Rochmont!" The soft, almost childlike voice was

unmistakable. "And Lady Constance too! What a delight to see you. And let me offer you my very best wishes. Few ladies are as fortunate in their choice of husbands."

Those words were addressed to me, but the special smile on Lady Antony's face was only for Rochmont. Neither so much as hinted that they had already encountered each other earlier in the day.

Being engaged to Lord Rochmont was becoming even less enjoyable than plotting my escape from the likes of Lord Bamwell. I plastered my best social smile on my face and soldiered on through what seemed to be an interminable afternoon.

My betrothed returned me to Hatton House without mishap and without the slightest hint of a romantic gesture. It was just as well. I was suffering a throbbing headache.

I escaped to my room where I lay down with a soft cloth dampened in lavender water pressed to my aching forehead. I knew it was important for me to regain my composure before venturing out again in public, with or without that magnet for beautiful widows, my own fiancé, Lord Rochmont.

Not that I could fault his behavior. Lady Edmund Norham and Lady Antony Compton had just been the most blatant in their expressions of joy at his appearance. There had been other signals, too numerous to count: flutterings of eyelashes, the brushing of gloved hands on his arm, and whispered asides for his ears only. Through it all, I had noticed no reciprocity from Rochmont. But then, I had not trusted myself to look his way all that often.

I stopped trying to understand my inscrutable fiancé and turned my thoughts to the two widows. That either was acquainted with Rochmont was no surprise. The late Lord Antony Compton had been the leader of a sporting set Rochmont was a part of whenever he was in England. It followed naturally that he would have met the beauteous Madeleine from time to time before her husband's demise— and who knew how many times since?

It was also easy to explain his acquaintance with Lady

Norham. She was, as he, a child born into the French aristocracy prior to the Revolution, and had been brought to England by parents fleeing The Terror.

As the cool compress began to relieve the pounding in my
brain, I considered the tidbits that I had heard about her. At a
young age, she had wed Sir Edmund Norham, an English
diplomat who acted as liaison with various factions of the
exiled Bourbon court. He had been the most satisfactory of
older husbands, dying within six weeks of the wedding,
leaving his widow a fortune that not even her expensive
tastes had exhausted.

The previous spring, while international society gathered
in Brussels awaiting the confrontation between Wellington
and Boney, her name had been linked with half the field
level officers of the Allied countries. After the Allied occu-
pation of Paris, she had worked her way through the other
half. But it seemed she had still found time for my brother
Jack, who was a very junior officer. Clearly, she also had
found time for my fiancé.

There was a scratch on the door, and Daisy entered,
flushed and out of breath, bearing an exquisite bouquet of
lilies of the valley and a note that read:

Dear Constance,
A thousand apologies for not taking leave of you in
person, but time does not permit. I must needs be from
London for a week or two. I do loathe these interruptions.
                    Yours faithfully,
                            Blaise
P.S. You need not concern yourself for Daisy in the
meantime; Armand goes with me.

Now there were two of us flushed and out of breath.

The fragrance of the little white flowers filled the room,
reminding me of the note. "These interruptions," "Yours
faithfully"; the two phrases played over and over in my
mind. If they meant anything at all, what possibly could

have been so urgent that he could not have spared thirty or forty minutes to stop by Hatton House to say good-bye in person? But what would he have said—or done—if he had bid me farewell in person? Would I, for once, have kept the sort of cordial, yet correct composure that I wished to maintain with him? I stared at the diamond he had placed on my ring finger. Its facets winked back at me, catching the late sun's rays. Well, Constance, I told myself, think of it as a reprieve. If you wish to make Major Howells your devoted swain, you had better get busy. But instead of making a definite plan of action, I reread Rochmont's note and tucked it into the drawer in my bedside table.

The next morning I awoke surrounded by the fragrance of lilies of the valley. Of course, their fragrance reminded me of Rochmont, but I steadfastly resisted the urge to remove his missive from my bedside table and reread it. To what purpose? I had memorized every word.

When I entered the breakfast room, Papa was reading what I supposed to be important government papers. Jack was solving the problem posed by Cook's enormous selection of dishes on the sideboard, by taking a generous portion of everything. I helped myself to a buttered egg, toast, and a cup of tea. I knew better than to so much as greet Papa, who was not to be disturbed while he was engaged in serious matters.

But either my presence penetrated his concentration or he had completed his reading.

"Constance, my dear, how well you are looking. And Jack, my boy," he added as he removed his reading glasses, "if you can find the time, do stop by my study after luncheon. I believe that you might be of some small service to your country, if you put your mind to it."

Papa exited, leaving me open-mouthed in astonishment and Jack with a satisfied smirk.

"Now that England no longer needs you for cannon fodder, what possible use can you be to our esteemed Regent's government?" I enquired of my brother.

"Connie, your lack of faith in me cuts me to the core,"

Jack protested between bites of ham. "Our sire is convinced that I have a future as a diplomat."

"Ah, dancing with the wives of ambassadors, entertaining foreign princes at clubs and sporting events—I suppose Papa recognizes talent when he sees it." I admitted.

"Been training for just such a vocation since I was but a lad." Jack managed to sound as if his dedication to his own pleasure was the greatest of virtues.

"I met someone yesterday who expressed delight in meeting Captain Jack Hatton's sister."

Jack did not look up from his plate. Such a message did not constitute real news.

"A Lady Edmund Norham, newly arrived from Paris, I believe."

Jack's fork hesitated for a second on its way from plate to mouth.

"The Fair Thérèse," Jack rolled his eyes and favored me with a roguish smile. "I wonder what brings her to London?"

"What is to wonder about? From her reaction, I assume her presence in London has something to do with a very close relative of mine, who happens to be eating breakfast at this very table." I fixed Jack with my best penetrating stare.

Jack shrugged. "You will lose if you bet on that proposition. Younger sons are not that lady's favorites. Whatever her purpose in coming to London, does not include yours truly. Old Norham left her pretty well set, but with her spending habits, new infusions of the ready are always welcome. By the by . . . where did you chance to meet her? She is not much for ladies' visiting hours and come-out balls."

I schooled my face to betray no concern. "Rochmont and I encountered her yesterday in the park."

"More like she accosted Rochmont, if I know Lady N.! She has been after him for ages." He caught himself before saying more, as solemn a look as I had ever seen on his face.

"Connie, my dear, I do not know how you managed to engage Rochmont's interest and, believe me, I do wish you happiness with him, but unless you want to be kept on tenterhooks for the rest of your days, you will have to learn to take the Lady Norhams in stride."

"Much as your intended will have to, I suppose." I was feeling much too fragile to pursue the topic. "However that may be," I added affecting nonchalance, "Lady Norham traveled to London in vain if she wishes to spend time with Rochmont for the next few days. He has been called out of town on urgent business. I am listening for the sound of discreet wailing from certain widows."

"Speaking of widows, I hear the glorious Madeleine has returned to society. Is she not one of your particular friends, Connie?"

Now who was acting nonchalant? Jack concentrated on peeling an orange in an unbroken spiral as he spoke.

He must have known Lady Antony and I were hardly bosom friends, but it occurred to me that if Jack attracted her attention, she would have less time to devote to Rochmont. I tucked that thought away as quickly as it formed, and told myself I wished to be a good sister.

"She was riding in the park yesterday. Although gentlemen were ten-deep around her, I have confidence that you could manage to catch her attention, if you set your mind to it."

Then, remembering Rochmont's absence, I thought I would catch Jack while he was feeling positively disposed toward me. "Actually, I am quite certain that she will be at Almack's, and I could use an escort, what with Rochmont being unavailable."

Jack shrugged. "Why not? Intended to drag Rick there anyway. He's thinking about becoming a man of property and finding a wife. Although how he will deal with all those simpering misses in white muslin, I cannot imagine."

He popped the last segment of orange in his mouth, rose and bid me good day, with a brotherly pat on the shoulder.

I poured myself another cup of tea and took stock of matters, feeling quite pleased with the way things had arranged themselves. I would have the escort services of a much-

admired man about town. The object of my plan, Major
Howells, would evidently be in our party, and Jack intended
to pursue Lady Antony Compton, who had shown discom-
forting interest in my fiancé. It looked as if the future might
hold some pleasing possibilities.

Chapter Five

My choice of gown for that evening required careful consideration. Almack's is unfailingly filled with fresh young misses in white or pale pastels. One no longer in her first blush of youth is presented with a serious dilemma. To follow their example is to risk being called mutton dressed as lamb. To depart from their example is to draw attention to the number of one's seasons. But in the end, I was satisfied with my solution to this problem. I chose a silk crepe, just a shade or two deeper than sky blue, and accessorized it with a few strands and eardrops of pearls. I must confess that the color blue does not excite me. I find blue rather boring. Is there any mama of a blonde, blue-eyed daughter who does not swath her angel in blue from the cradle on? Certainly my dear mama had. But I have observed that most men, especially conventional men, seem to prefer the color, and I judged Major Howells to be—of all men—conventional.

I knew I had chosen wisely when I entered the drawing room where Jack and Major Howells awaited Mama and me before our departure for Almack's.

"Major Howells."

I extended my white-gloved hand to him. As he bowed to kiss the air over my fingers, I noticed a small patch of pink skin shining through the crown of his head. Was he going bald? Would he adopt that off-putting habit of combing-over sparse strands to hide his baldness?

"Lady Constance."

Was that faint flush on his face the result of his slight bow, or was it because of his proximity to my décolletage as he bowed?

"How kind you are to assist Jack in escorting Mama and me this evening!"

I treated him to my most radiant smile and rationed myself to two slow bats of my lashes. This time, I detected a tiny flush spreading up from his cravat across his freshly shaven face. Safe, solid Major Howells was going to be too, too easy to attach.

"I assure you, Lady Constance, it is an honor and a pleasure to be in your company," Major Howells responded solemnly.

Perhaps the process of making the good major my devoted swain was not going to be too easy, if this exchange was all I could expect from him in the way of sparkling conversation.

Across the room, I saw Jack's eyes narrowing speculatively. I would have to watch myself. Jack's first priority might be his own pleasure, but his powers of observation are acute. I did not need to ponder the matter to know that Jack, for all his scheming ways, would heartily disapprove of my plans for Major Howells.

Mama was also anything but helpful. Having at last seen the announcement of my engagement in *The Gazette,* she was applying her matchmaking to others. And for Mama, the first, and most vital step in arranging any match, is establishing the pedigree and connections of the objects of her assistance.

Poor Major Howells. All the way to Almack's, Mama quizzed him about his antecedents. She had scarcely settled herself in the carriage, the major seated beside her and across from Jack and me, when her inquiry began.

"Ah, Major," Mama inclined her plumed turban toward him, "how delighted I am that Jack has made the acquaintance of such a distinguished military man."

"You are too generous, Lady Chase," Major Howells replied feelingly.

Mama's plumes swayed as she nodded. The major had passed her first test. She approved of proper deference from those she chose to favor with her notice.

"Howells, Howells," Mama mused, tapping her fan gently against her chin. "I seem to remember that there was a Howells family in West Sussex with a fine military tradition. Now let me think . . . the eldest son was some years my senior . . . was a friend of my cousin Frederick . . . who was a great chum of my older sister Anne . . . who came out the year of the girl who married the Howells lad. Sarah! Sarah Hewitt of the Hampshire Hewitts! Is she, by any chance your Mama?"

"I am sorry, Lady Chase," the major sounded genuinely regretful, "but my mother was not of the Hampshire Hewitts. She was a Trabert of the Lincolnshire Traberts."

"Trabert," Mama repeated the name consideringly. "Was not that the name of the ginger haired girl who married Tommy Barnet-Smythe last summer, Constance?"

"No, Mama, her name was Tolbert, Frances Tolbert, and she was from Leicestershire."

Mama paused for a moment to regroup her forces. A first class interrogator does not give up so easily. She redirected her attention to the longsuffering major.

"It is difficult for me to believe, Major Howells, with your military prowess, that you are not related in some way to the Howells of West Sussex. Aptitudes, I am convinced, are inherited. Which, of course is why it is essential that people of superior birth be given the responsibility for running the government."

I refrained from mentioning Prinny and the coterie of sycophants who surrounded him. It was all Papa and his associates could do to rescue England from their machinations.

"I think it would be a good idea for you to look into the possibility that there is a connection, Major." Perseverance is one of Mama's chief virtues. "Do write your father. There must be a distant cousinship of some sort."

"I regret, Lady Chase, that my father has been deceased these twenty years. But I will search through family papers to see if I have overlooked a possible clue."

It was the best the beleaguered Major Howells could do. After all, he was trained for soldiering, not diplomacy. But being a man of fortitude, he refrained from an audible sigh of relief when our carriage pulled up to Almack's.

Whatever discomfort Major Howells had suffered during Mama's inquisition must have been partially compensated for by the welcome he and Jack received from all seven of Almack's Patronesses. As might be anticipated, Lady Jersey was first to spy my two eligible escorts. Jack, in spite of his rare appearances at the ultimate pinnacle of the Marriage Mart, needed no introduction. And no recriminations over his long absence were given.

Major Howells, even though previously an unknown, received a welcome fit for royalty. By what method news of a marriageable man's fortune spreads throughout the *ton* is a mystery to me, but it was clear from the Patronesses' kind smiles and greetings, the lavishness of the nabob uncle's bequest to the major was known.

I knew I must act quickly if I meant to secure anything but a country dance with the major before an endless parade of fresh young misses was presented for his inspection.

Between the effusions of Ladies Jersey and Cowper, I managed to say in a forlorn voice, "Congratulations, Major, you will be a veritable social lion before this evening is over. I suppose the waltz I had so looked forward to is now beyond my expectation."

What could a proper gentleman say in response? I was able to scratch in Major Howells' name for the first waltz before each of us was deluged with prospective partners.

The evening had not progressed very far when it was apparent that my newly engaged status had made me a favorite with gentlemen of birth and fortune attempting to avoid the very young ladies who were so eager to attract their atten-

tion. As a betrothed lady, I was a safe island in a sea of potential predators. Lord Cathcart, heir to the Duke of Barham,
The Honorourable Alastair Plinkindon, Mr. Ferdinand
Courlan, and Lord Stillwell were only the most notable of
the hotly pursued who were all too happy to dance with me
and avoid the blandishments of Patronesses, Mamas and
their prettily behaved but single minded charges.

As I danced with one partner after another, I noticed
Drusilla Fortesque sitting on the sidelines next to her Great
Aunt Louisa. Other unclaimed ladies had a desperate, de-
spairing air about them. Not so Miss Fortesque. She gazed
on the frothy scene with an expression of amused detachment. Her gown, a moss green creation, was out of the ordinary, to put it kindly.

The cut reflected the art of a skilled London modiste. But
the neckline, which was designed with sufficient décolletage
to reveal Miss Fortesque's considerable charms, was filled
with layers of lace that might have seen previous use as
boudoir curtains. I made a mental note to do what I could to
see that she did not sit out the entire evening. But then I remembered that I really did need to attend to executing my
own plans.

When Major Howells approached me for our waltz, his
look of pleased relief was apparent. Evidently, answering
the inquiries and parrying the sallies of eighteen-year-old
young ladies was almost as wearing as being the object of an
interrogation by Mama.

In all candor, I must confess that waltzing with the good
major was less like floating over the dance floor than it was
like taking part in a military drill. Instead of turning us in
graceful circles, Major Howells tended to direct us more in
squared-off corners. The sight of Jack and Lady Antony
dancing effortlessly across the ballroom from where the
good major and I labored tempted me to envy.

But before I could descend into total misery, my attention
was caught by—what can I say? A truly stunning couple!
Poor, unfortunate Miss Fortesque! She had caught the atten-

tion of Lord Bamwell! A glance to where her Great Aunt Louisa sat told the whole sad story. Mrs. Fortesque was watching the trial of her great niece with a look of supreme satisfaction. Louisa Fortesque intended to promote a match between the unconventional Drusilla and that pompous oaf. A wave of disgust washed over me.

"I say Lady Constance," my partner inquired, "are you feeling unwell? Did I, perchance tread on you?" The worried look on Major Howells' face required sincerest reassurances.

I silently scolded myself as I used the time remaining to me to concentrate my most charming attention where it belonged, upon my partner. This was the second time in one evening that I had let my mind wander in his presence, when I should have been devoting all my energies to making myself agreeable to him. But old habits are hard to break. It occurred to me that Major Howells and Miss Fortesque might make a good match. I could perform the necessary introduction myself, and with the major's punctilious good manners, he would ask Drusilla to dance.

Before I could stop myself I said, "Major Howells, I have a delightful friend whom I am sure you would enjoy meeting."

What harm could it do? I had already danced my one permitted dance with Major Howells, and both he and Miss Fortesque seemed to me to be in need of rescuing.

The evening wound on its weary way as evenings at Almack's tend to do for those not in their first encounter with London society. During the carriage ride home, Mama mercifully did not continue her exploration of Major Howells' antecedents. I was therefore able to maneuver an invitation from Major Howells to escort me for a ride in the park the following afternoon. As I anticipated, Jack had already secured Lady Antony's company for that important hour of seeing and being seen. He surprised me by suggesting that we make it a foursome. Evidently, his relationship with Lady Antony had not progressed to the stage where he was determined to have her company exclusively to himself.

* * *

We were quite the dashing quartet as we made our way to the park the next afternoon. Jack, on his strong and steady roan gelding, Soldier, and Lady Antony, on her pretty bay mare, Marvel, led. Major Howells and I followed. After arriving at the park, it was not long before we were swallowed up in the crush. Lady Antony was quickly surrounded by admirers. Jack, apparently untroubled by a multiplicity of rivals, turned his attention to a discussion of a sale at Tattersall's that promised some excellent cattle for those with sufficient means. Major Howells, who certainly met those qualifications and wanted to build a respectable stable, joined in.

Knowing that Jack and Major Howells would be engrossed until it was time to leave, I decided to have a chat with Freddie Stanhope and Charlie Stockton, whom I had spied some distance away. They were unfailingly amusing and could be counted upon to be current with the latest news. Had they been ladies, they would have been called gossips. But as gentlemen, they were simply well-informed sources of information.

Before I had progressed very far in their direction, someone hailed me. Lady Norham, attired in a habit and hat that exactly matched her caramel eyes, trotted up to me on a showy chestnut mare.

"Lady Constance, but what a delight to encounter you," she exclaimed in heavy accents.

She smiled charmingly, all the while scrutinizing every inch of my person, attire, mount and equipage. I had no doubt that Serena, my steady gray mare, could tolerate close inspection. And I knew my navy blue habit with its jabot of snowy lace and my pert little navy hat, sporting a feather that curved by my left cheek, were flawless.

But her conversation was not about either my mount or my attire.

"Where is Monsieur le Marquis? One would not think that he would wish to lose the opportunity to be seen with so lovely a promised bride!"

The truth, of course, was that I had no idea where Monsieur le Marquis was. But I had no intention of admitting that small fact to my inquisitor.

"Rochmont leads a busy life, as do I. I certainly do not require his constant attendance on me. I cannot think such an arrangement would be all that convenient."

I was pleased with the bored tone in my voice.

Lady Norham tilted her head and narrowed her eyes.

"Can it be that Rochmont has gotten himself engaged to a lady who is truly indifferent to him? Somehow, I find that difficult to believe. Or has he simply not bothered to try to attach you, Lady Constance? But that does not answer either. I have never known him to need to try all that much. But you are so . . . what is the word . . . not young, exactly. So very English, perhaps."

She gave a little nod as if satisfied with this pronouncement.

"I wonder how you shall manage with such a one as a husband?"

I found myself in complete agreement with Lady Norham. Not only did I wonder how I would manage with a husband such as Rochmont, I was determined to avoid the necessity of finding out. But I kept that fact to myself. She gave a little shrug of dismissal.

"At any event, my dear, your detachment, genuine or affected, is a wise course. I would wager that you have no idea where or with whom your intended is. You might as well become accustomed to such a state of affairs . . . Oh! What an unfortunate choice of words! I do beg your pardon! Forgive me, Lady Constance, there is Lord Seldon, and I did wish to speak with him."

A distant roll of thunder expressed my feelings as Lady Norham departed.

The usually reliable Freddie Stanhope and Charlie Stockton failed to lift my spirits. Prinny's ailments had never intrigued me, but Freddie and Charlie were full of the details of our regent's latest complaint. The only saving factor was that it involved headaches rather than intestinal distress. Other tidbits were no more delightful. Not only had Brummel been forced by his debts to flee to the Continent, it was my informants' considered opinion that his return was unlikely.

How depressing! Never having been bitten by the gambling fever, it was difficult for me to understand the grip it had on the *ton*. And while the Beau's wit could sting, he always lent sparkle to an evening—in more ways than one. I felt nothing but admiration for a man who almost single-handedly had brought clean linen into fashion!

And, according to Freddie and Charlie, Lord Byron had once more departed our shores for warmer climes. This certainly could be no surprise. His scorn for England and all things English was apparent. But the scandals he had generated had always been diverting. Now we would have to await news of them to come to us from a distance.

With another roll of thunder, Jack rode up and announced he and the major were anxious to get Lady Antony and me home before the storm hit.

We were almost in sight of Hatton House when a disturbance at the side of the street caught our attention. A fight of sorts was ensuing between two unlikely combatants: a young lady and a street urchin. A crowd had gathered and advice was being shouted to the adversaries. The young lady wielded a furled parasol, attempting to strike the urchin. Markedly quick on his feet, he eluded blows from the parasol, while aiming stones at a small animal that more resembled a dirty mop than a dog. The lady ordered the urchin to stop attacking the "poor creature". The urchin answered profanely that the "monster" deserved to die for its crime. A maid stood nearby, alternately wringing her hands and hiding her eyes.

Jack immediately took control of the situation. Asking Major Howells to accompany Lady Antony home and tossing Soldier's reigns to me, he dismounted and brought the altercation to a halt by flinging a handful of coins in the direction of the blasphemous urchin, who, being as agile of mind as of body, scooped up the coins and departed with alacrity.

Unhappily, the young lady did not approve of this resolution to the conflict. She turned on Jack, flushed with her exertions.

"How could you do such a thing! Rewarding that malefactor! Now he has escaped, and you will never catch him!"

Her bonnet had come loose and hung on her back, attached only by a knotted ribbon that looked none too secure. Luxuriant mahogany-colored hair was threatening to fall out of a chignon caught at the back of her head. Gold flecks in her brown eyes sparkled with fury as she remonstrated with my brother.

He favored her with his famous lopsided grin. "I daresay I could not catch the little bas . . . rascal. And I do not intend to try."

"But what a terrible lesson to have taught him! To escape scot-free, and to actually realize financial gain instead of punishment when he cruelly and ruthlessly persecuted a helpless creature just because it had taken a little bite of his meat pie!"

When the young lady was forced to stop for breath, attention shifted to the living mop. With unfortunate timing, the mop chose that moment to extend a pink tongue and lick off a remaining crumb of meat pie from its black button nose. Even though its eyes were hidden under dirty grey hair, it had an insouciant air as it sat, apparently assessing Jack— not an appropriate attitude for a recently rescued beast.

I decided the time had come for me to intervene.

"Miss Fortesque," for that indeed was the name of the gentle lady still darting angry glances at Jack. "Permit me to present my brother, Captain John Hatton, late of Britain's occupying forces in Paris."

Jack executed an elegant bow, his famous grin once more in evidence.

"Jack, may I present Miss Drusilla Fortesque, recently of Bath."

Miss Fortesque's curtsey was no less elegant than Jack's bow.

At that moment, the promised deluge was released. I suggested Miss Fortesque and her maid might wish to go with us to Hatton House, for not only would they be drenched if they continued on to her aunt's, Miss Fortesque would want to repair her appearance and her gown before facing her Great Aunt Louisa.

As we began to make our way home, Miss Fortesque scooped up the dog, whose dirty coat was rapidly turning to mud.

"Miss Fortesque! You certainly do not intend to take that mongrel with you!" Jack objected.

"Captain Hatton!" Miss Fortesque returned mockingly, "I most certainly do and I most certainly will!"

She punctuated this declaration by placing a kiss on the creature's soggy head and calling it a "dear doggy".

A choking sound issued from Jack's direction.

Chapter Six

When we arrived at Hatton House, the dog was dispatched to the stables along with the horses. Jack gave orders that the "dam . . . dashed mongrel" be thoroughly scrubbed. Miss Fortesque gave orders that it be treated with great care, since it had suffered considerably and would likely be frightened if not spoken to gently. Jack said perhaps it numbered a terrier among its antecedents and might earn its keep attacking the rat population. Miss Fortesque suggested cook might have a bone for the "sweet darling" to chew on. Jack raised an eyebrow, but restrained himself from commenting further.

I shepherded Miss Fortesque into the house before she and Jack could issue any further contradictory instructions to a bewildered stable lad, delivered both Miss Fortesque and her maid into Daisy's care, and sent a note round to Mrs. Fortesque informing her that her niece had taken shelter at Hatton House. Since Miss Fortesque's gown was soaking wet and torn, it was clear that some time would be needed to render it wearable.

Finding a gown for Miss Fortesque to wear in the meantime was a challenge. Even though I am certainly not flat-chested, Miss Fortesque's endowment is noticeably more generous than mine. The problem was finding something for her that was both decent and permitted her to breathe. Finally, Daisy hit on the happy solution of leaving some strategic fasteners undone on the back of a bronze silk and covering that omission with a green and gold paisley shawl, which was to be kept tightly secured at all costs. A deeper hem was quickly basted to keep the gown from pooling about Miss Fortesque's feet. When these tasks were completed, I was struck by her distinctive appearance. With her hair pulled into a double looped chignon, one's attention was drawn to her warm, gold-flecked eyes, finely arched brows, and rich, Devonshire cream complexion. My first impression of Drusilla Fortesque as a plain, dowdy miss had been quite mistaken.

When we arrived at the drawing room, Jack was already there, looking out the window at the storm and sipping a drink stronger than the tea I had ordered.

"Miss Fortesque," he said appreciatively, "if that is one of Connie's gowns, she must make a gift of it to you. I cannot believe it suits her half as well as it does you, and she would be reminded of that fact whenever she put it on."

If Jack thought to fluster our guest with his flattery, he was to be disappointed. Miss Fortesque dismissed his suggestion as "nonsense", but did take the opportunity to thank him civilly for coming to her rescue.

"I am most indebted to you, Captain Hatton, and I am very much ashamed if, in the heat of the moment, I sounded critical or ungrateful."

The words were correct, but something in Miss Fortesque's tone and demeanor failed to reflect the degree of gratitude that my brother habitually receives for the smallest of services rendered to members of the fair sex.

"Neither ungrateful nor overly critical, Miss Fortesque, just very clear about your priorities."

"Oh dear," she laughed her contralto laugh. "I fear I am all too often quite sure of, not only what I, but what everybody else should be doing. I grew up in an all female household, and I never did learn proper deference to authority."

She did not sound as if she particularly cared to change her ways.

"And I have spent the past ten years in the Army, and have become accustomed to giving orders and having them obeyed. Encountering you, my dear Miss Fortesque, has provided excellent training for my return to civilian life."

My brother the diplomat! Perhaps he did have a future with the Foreign Office. Papa would be impressed.

A footman appeared with a heavily laden tea tray. But before he could make much progress toward the tea table, a flash streaked across the carpet and came to rest in front of Jack. Only the black nose and pink tongue provided clues to the creature's identity. It was stunningly white. White enough to satisfy the recently departed Beau Brummel in the matter of shirts and linen.

Miss Fortesque and I let out simultaneous squeals of delight. An unnerved footman made his cautious way with the tea tray and set it on the table in front of me. He regarded the white mop with disdain.

"Beg pardon, my lady, but that beast is more difficult to control than a greased pig. The stable lads could not keep it from running into the kitchen, and the scullery maid and boot boy were only able to keep it there for bathing by bribing it with a meal that would have filled a grown man! And it being a female too!" He blushed as he delivered this last bit of information.

I could scarcely maintain a straight face.

"She does seem to be content in her present surroundings. Apologize to the staff for the inconvenience she caused. We shall look after her now. And, thank you, Robert."

He looked relieved to bow and leave.

"A female. I should have known," Jack addressed the bundle of white yarn at his feet. "What shall we name you? You do not seem to be very fat, for all your prodigious appetite. On the whole, I believe it is your hairdo that is most distinctive. I have it! Medusa!"

"No! No! Too cruel! She has done nothing to deserve such a name!" Miss Fortesque's protests were heartfelt.

"Medora, call her Medora. That sounds so much nicer. And it is much more sympathetic."

"Wherever did you hear such a name?" Jack wondered.

"Miss Fortesque is reading *The Corsair*, Jack," I explained. "I am sure the name was there to pop into her mind, particularly as a substitute for something as dreadful as Medusa."

"Another of Byron's legion of devotees." The look Jack directed at Miss Fortesque was more scornful than a true diplomat would have permitted himself.

"Devotee is a bit strong, sir," she protested. "I am merely reading a poem he wrote. No doubt I am one of the last ladies in England to do so."

"No doubt you are profoundly saddened by his departure for the Continent," Jack countered.

"On the contrary! I think it is in the best interest for all concerned."

"But surely, you cannot like the idea of his escaping to live out his days in decadence."

"From what I understand, being in England hardly elevated his behavior. It just exposed him to more censure than he might have received elsewhere. And furthermore," Miss Fortesque was warming to a topic about which she seemed to have formed strong opinions. "Furthermore, his departure will remove him from vulnerable English ladies who apparently are determined to save him from himself."

"Are you telling me, Miss Fortesque, that you do not believe the love of a virtuous lady can reform a rake?"

Jack was genuinely amazed. After all, his own success with the opposite sex was enhanced by his reputation for naughtiness, if not the serious decadence of Lord Byron.

Our surprising guest laughed and shrugged. "I have no idea, Captain, for I have little first hand knowledge of rakes, Bath not being a favorite setting for them. But to place oneself in a role that is a combination of parson and governess to one who shows no interest in either religion or academics, seems to me to be an unconscionably foolish undertaking."

"So you do not believe that love conquers all, Miss Fortesque?"

"Whatever would make me believe such an unlikely proposition, Captain Hatton? Certainly nothing I have observed since arriving in London."

"I must confess to being quite disillusioned, ma'am. I had always thought that gently brought up English ladies were tenderhearted and idealistic, and quite ready to discover a finer, more sensitive side to their gentlemen friends than others had previously allowed."

Jack's smile said *he* certainly found that ladies of *his* acquaintance would overlook a great deal in order to give *him* the benefit of any doubt.

Miss Fortesque chuckled. "I do believe Captain Hatton, the idea that young ladies would adopt the practice of following their heads rather than their hearts, quite alarms you."

"*Touché*, Miss Fortesque," Jack sketched a bow in her direction. "Do promise me that you will not attempt to convert any of your sisters to your point of view."

"You have no cause for concern, Captain. I have said I have no taste for the role of either parson or governess. I think you are safe."

"I cannot tell you how happy your reassurance makes me. It has been a pleasure meeting you, Miss Fortesque, quite memorable, in fact."

"Thank you so much, Captain, for coming to the rescue. I promise to try to keep my alarming ideas to myself in the future."

"One can only hope that you fail in your promise, Miss Fortesque. The afternoon has been quite entertaining." Jack favored her again with his lopsided smile, bowed, and departed.

"Lady Constance!" Miss Fortesque turned to me in dismay. "Whatever can you be thinking? I really do not make it a habit to be so appallingly candid in expressing my opinions! I do apologize!"

I laughed. "Please do nothing of the sort. Jack has that effect on people. He positively dotes on leading one to say outrageous things. You stood up to him nicely, and it is unusual when any lady does. He might have been surprised, but I am certain he was pleased too. It must be boring to always have the opposite gender fawn and agree with everything one says."

"I should imagine you know that first hand, Lady Constance."

Such an idea startled me. How much had changed in the short time since that fateful encounter in the Sandforth's library. A pair of inscrutable black-brown eyes appeared unbidden in my mind's eye. I could not imagine a time when they would ever regard me without a certain reserve and objectivity. Why did that fact matter to me? Why did others' adoration mean so little and his lack of it mean so much? I refused to examine that particular question. I shrugged and smiled ruefully.

"I suppose one is bound to undervalue what comes too easily, Miss Fortesque."

"Would you mind terribly calling me Drusilla? I find 'Miss Fortesque' rather cumbersome."

"And you must call me Constance."

Since we were now on such informal footing, I decided I might compromise discretion in favor of discovering as much as I could about my new friend's reaction to her dancing partners of the previous evening. I salved my conscience when it rebuked me for being too intrusive by reminding it that Miss Fortesque—Drusilla—had shown herself to be quite capable of protecting her own interests in the art of verbal combat. If she could hold her own with Jack, I would present no challenge at all.

"I hope you enjoyed your evening at Almack's, Drusilla." I began my probe with a perfectly unexceptionable inquiry, as I idly fed scraps from the tea table to Medora, who sat on the sofa between my guest and me.

"Most entertaining!" Her enthusiasm seemed genuine.

"Having heard so much about Almack's, its inflexible rules, overbearing Patronesses, hordes of fresh young misses, not to mention its so-called refreshments of stale cakes and warm orangeat, I must confess that my expectations were modest. But the performance of those in attendance was diverting beyond anything I have witnessed, even during promenade hour in the Pump Room!"

"Did I see you dancing with Lord Bamwell?" A silly question. Given his lack of dancing ability, only the most dedicated gamblers in the card room had not observed Drusilla dancing with Lord Bamwell. But being a lady, she refrained from reminding me of that fact.

"I fear you did," Drusilla responded. "Great Aunt Louisa was determined to bring me to his attention. When she was able to attract his notice, her happiness knew no bounds. During the carriage ride home, all she could do was exclaim about my good fortune. 'Such condescension', she kept saying of the fact that he had asked me to dance." Drusilla's laugh was almost a giggle. "That description of his manners, at least, was apt. But I understand that before the announcement of your betrothal to Lord Rochmont, Lord Bamwell had entertained hopes of making you his bride. So in a very real way, by taking any notice of me at all, he is truly lowering his sights."

"Nonsense!" I replied feelingly. "I confess, though, to a concern for you if your great aunt and Lord Bamwell come to an agreement that you are the best candidate for mama of his young daughters and mother of his heir! It is a fate I would not wish on a friend."

"So that was the reason why you presented me to your devoted Major Howells. I thought as much. But, please do not waste any energy worrying about my being forced into a marriage with Lord Bamwell. I believe it is only grand heiresses and daughters of noble debtors who ultimately must submit to having the wedding service read over them against their will. And I have the good fortune of being neither!"

"Oh dear, was I so obvious?"

I did feel somewhat chagrined that my unselfish impulse of the previous evening had been so lacking in both subtly and necessity. "But are you quite certain that Mrs. Fortesque and Lord Bamwell together cannot apply considerable pressure if they are in agreement about your marrying him?"

Drusilla dismissed my concern with an airy wave.

"Great Aunt Louisa imagines that she 'rescued' me from my maternal relations in Bath, but nothing could be further from the truth. Indeed, I have every intention of returning to them when my London season is over. My circumstances may be modest, but they are in no way desperate."

I knew a twinge of what I might have called jealousy, if such a thought were not ludicrous. To have contentment with as modest a lot in life as was Drusilla Fortesque's seemed to me to be a happy state indeed. But it was difficult to imagine a lady of her wit and spirits contemplating so limited a future.

"I must admit to finding your attitude admirable, Drusilla," I began cautiously, offering a bite of smoked salmon to Medora, who showed a marked preference for salmon over cucumber. "But do you not ever dream of establishing a home of your own with a husband who dotes on you?"

"Really, Constance, how naïve do you think I am?" Drusilla's throaty laughter took any sting out of her question. "Indeed, I am not at all certain I could bear such doglike devotion in a gentleman! And be honest! It is not the dependable, devoted Major Howells to whom you are engaged, but the tough minded Lord Rochmont. And I must say, I respect your choice in the matter. I suspect you understand that, in no time at all, you would ride roughshod over the good Major, utterly destroying the most essential element of respect that a wife must feel for her husband. And, although I have never had the occasion to become acquainted with Lord Rochmont, his reputation is such, I believe not even you, with all your wit and charm, would be able to ride roughshod over him."

I knew what Drusilla said was true, and that was precisely my problem. But it was impossible to as much as hint that my engagement was unwanted, because she believed me to have chosen Rochmont for sound reasons, an impression I did not wish to destroy. I was uncertain how to respond to her observation that Major Howells was "devoted" to me. Gaining his devotion had indeed been my goal, but hearing it as fact from a neutral observer gave me pause.

I smiled a knowing smile, acknowledging my wisdom in choosing the likes of Rochmont as my prospective husband, but challenged her impression about Major Howells.

"Major Howells is an admirable gentleman, Drusilla, but I am certain you overstate matters when you describe him as being devoted to me. I do believe that he is simply grateful to have a lady known to society who is willing to smooth the way for him."

"Perhaps you are right," she allowed. "After all, our acquaintance with you is just about all Major Howells and I have in common, and he is not the easiest of conversationalists."

I could not argue with her assessment.

"Anyway," she added, "how Major Howells feels toward you is irrelevant because you are engaged to Lord Rochmont, and I cannot imagine your being so cruel as to encourage Major Howells to have any warmer regard for you than friendship. And I certainly cannot imagine someone with the reputation of Lord Rochmont being complacent about his intended setting up a serious flirtation."

I fed Medora a macaroon and fought the shame that settled over me on hearing Drusilla's words.

The footman's announcement that Daisy had finished repairs of Miss Fortesque's gown offered a welcome distraction.

"Thank you very much for your very kind hospitality after Captain Hatton's timely rescue," Drusilla said feelingly as she rose to leave. "I will take Medora with me now. I fear she is making herself very much at home."

The little dog was eying the last macaroon on the tea tray, showing no interest in her new mistress' imminent departure.

I discovered that I was loath to let Medora depart. I needed a diversion.

"Let her stay," I asked earnestly. "She seems to have settled in quite nicely."

What cook would think of having a canine as a major consumer of her endeavors I did not want to consider.

"I cannot ask you to help care for her," Drusilla protested. "I have already caused quite enough disruption of your household by rescuing her."

"I seem to remember your Great Aunt Louisa has a tortoise-shell tabby that might not be too pleased to share her domain with a little white dog."

"Bella!" Drusilla cried in dismay. "I had forgotten all about her. She is so much like part of the furniture, after all. What could I have been thinking?"

And so it was decided that Medora would stay with me. I promised that Jack would not be permitted to consign her to the stables and urged Miss Fortesque to visit as frequently as she wished.

Daisy was elated. She had seen the little dog below stairs, but no one had listened to her insistence that the poor little thing needed to have its hair brushed out of its eyes. She remedied the problem, applying my second-best brush to Medora.

"I'm sure you won't mind, my lady. You really don't need two hair brushes anyway, do you?" Nor did it seem I needed the pink satin ribbon Daisy used to fasten a topknot, revealing Medora's shiny black eyes that blinked when exposed to the light. Gazing about my dressing room, and apparently deciding it just might meet her standards, the little dog curled up on a chair cushion and went to sleep.

Thinking to follow her example, I asked Daisy to close

the curtains and I retired for a nap. But weary as I was, sleep, not even restful relaxation would come. Lady Norham's face kept coming to mind, along with her words. "I would wager you have no idea where he is or with whom." *True. Too true.* "It is just as well that you appear detached, whether genuine or affected." What choice did I have? I suspected that Lady Norham knew my betrothed very well indeed, and she clearly thought I was too naïve and inexperienced to engage his interest. I reminded myself that it did not matter what Rochmont thought of me. I would find a substitute fiancé for him as soon as possible.

Drusilla's confidence in my honor tore at my conscience. I knew I would never fall in love with Major Howells. What if Drusilla's first impression was correct, and he had developed a *tendre* for me. Had I not intended him to?

Drusilla was right. Attempting to attach Major Howell's affections had been cruel of me, and not at all honorable. I promised myself to make a serious effort to promote a match between the major and Drusilla. She was courageous to face her confined expectations with such aplomb, but she deserved better. And as Major Howells' wife, she would have a secure place in society and enjoy financial ease. I could think of no young lady more worthy of such blessings.

My room was still filled with the fragrance of lilies of the valley. They would not last much longer—certainly not as long as it would take Lord Rochmont to return from wherever he had gone. If I wished to keep them, they would have to be pressed. In my mind's eye, I could see Lady Norham scoff at such an idea. Daisy would understand, though. Was I as silly and green as Daisy?

I extracted the note from its hiding place. "I do loathe these interruptions." "Yours faithfully." I was a fool to attach any special meaning beyond courtesy to those words. Even Drusilla Fortesque, whose company and wit I enjoyed, would caution me against putting any trust in them. I looked down at the diamond on my hand. Even in the shadowed room, it caught a few rays of light and winked back at me.

"A diamond of the first water for a diamond of the first water."

That was all I knew for certain about my betrothed's feelings for me. I had better remember that.

Chapter Seven

The next day's visiting hour brought its usual crush to Hatton House. The Duchess of Fanshawe's masked ball was the most important topic of conversation. Each year there was discussion about whether disguises lowered the level of decorum and invited breaches of desirable behavior. Each year the highest sticklers deplored the *ton's* nearly unanimous decision to attend. Each year there was sufficient decorum that the ball was not pronounced bad *ton*. On the other hand, each year the ball produced sufficient gossip that one could not afford to miss it. The duchess wisely timed her ball just after the first wave of come-out balls when society was wearying of perfect behavior, but before the season's inevitable scandals had developed. The diversion of the masked ball was an antidote to the boredom that society abhorred.

Great energy was invested in costumes. Classical disguises provided respectable cover to uncover, so to speak. Favored suitors were sometimes given hints of ladies' disguises, so that happy pairs could appear as well known couples: Romeo and Juliet, Antony and Cleopatra, Heloise and Abelard. Servants, tailors and dressmakers supplemented their wages with hefty bribes to reveal the costumes of particular ladies and gentlemen.

"Lady Constance," Major Howells' face registered sincere concern. "I am a little confused. Is this masked ball really quite the thing? Do you plan to attend?"

"Certainly I will attend. It is a much tamer affair than some claim. In fact, I do believe that the duchess encourages the likes of Mrs. Fortesque to disapprove of it, just to be sure that there will be a sizable crowd."

I had expected my reassurance to erase the look of concern from Major Howells' face, but it became more severe. And then his familiar flush appeared.

"So, it is unlikely that Miss Fortesque will be in attendance?"

The major affected nonchalance, but acting was clearly not among his abilities. I tried to hide my satisfaction in his obvious interest in Drusilla. I could see my plan for her happy and secure future could be easily executed.

"I am so glad you have brought that problem to my attention, major. I shall set my mind to overcoming any objections Mrs. Fortesque might have to her great niece's presence at the ball. The disguises are quite harmless fun, really, and someone with Miss Fortesque's wit and discretion could be a valuable addition to the evening. Particularly if her disguise is known to a few gentleman who could act as a guarantee that she is not bothered by the small element attending with the intention of encouraging misbehavior."

Major Howells' cravat dipped as he swallowed. "Please, Lady Constance, let me know if there is anything I can do to reassure Mrs. Fortesque that Miss Fortesque does not need to have the slightest concern of insult or embarrassment."

"Depend upon it, Major. And thank you."

How satisfying to meet with instant cooperation when acting in another's best interest.

Things were going unbelievably well, for at that precise moment, Mrs. Fortesque and Miss Fortesque were announced, and Major Howells excused himself to greet them.

I had little opportunity, however, to bask in the furtherance of my plan. For Major Howells had no sooner left, than Lord Cathcart appeared.

"Ah, my dear Lady Constance! You do not mind if I sit here beside you, do you?"

The question was a formality. When one is heir to dukedom, and is handsome to the point of beauty, one is accustomed to being welcomed by all, particularly by the fair sex.

"Lord Cathcart," I acknowledged, with a slight nod, maintaining punctilious correctness as a shield against the put-downs for which he is notorious.

He draped himself over the opposite end of the sofa and examined me from head to toe through his quizzing glass.

Then he lowered the glass and gazed out upon the garden, offering me a view of his finely chiseled profile. The contours of his face were very like an Italian portrait of St. Michael the Archangel. The sunlight playing on his pale blonde hair even provided a convincing hint of a halo. But his blue-grey eyes were so cold, I would not have been surprised if frost suddenly appeared where his glance struck. Indeed, I felt a chill when his attention returned to me.

"Lilac," he motioned toward my gown, "not your usual choice, but rather becoming," a fulsome compliment, by Lord Cathcart's standards.

"Is it, by any chance, a sign of half-mourning for an absent fiancé?"

"Is that a robin in the tree over there?" I responded, also turning my gaze toward the window.

The sole acknowledgement Lord Cathcart made of my snub was the slight raising of his left eyebrow and the faintest of smiles.

"The Fanshawe Ball is upon us once more, my dear Lady Constance," he drawled in his perpetually bored tone. "Not that we can hope for anything truly shocking, but at least it will be a relief from these interminable come-outs."

He swung his quizzing glass idly as he spoke.

"Of course, one must give some thought to a costume. Quite tiresome if one does not pay sufficient attention to what others are wearing. Last year I went as Robin Hood."

He need not have reminded me. Who would ever forget

the sight of the old dowagers unable to take their eyes off
Lord Cathcart in skin-tight leggings that are standard for a
Robin Hood ensemble? Furthermore, who would ever forget
the appearance of so many Maid Marions?

"This year, I am considering going as Marc Antony."

Would not the dowagers be pleased.

He stopped swinging his quizzing glass, and once more
studied me through it.

"And I must say, my dear Lady Constance, I do believe
you would make a stunning Cleopatra."

"You flatter me, Lord Cathcart."

"Nonsense, my dear, I never flatter." He dropped the glass
once more, but did not cease studying me.

"A straight black wig, with a fringe, I think, and a little
kohl about the eyes, of course."

"I shall take the matter under consideration," I lied.

"Do that, Lady Constance."

Lord Cathcart, ever elegant and languid, rose to his feet
slowly, bowed over my hand, and proceeded to the far side
of the room just in time to avoid Miss Althea Sandforth, who
had spotted him chatting with me and was making her way
with determined speed in our direction.

"Lady Constance," Miss Sandforth, obviously torn between the requirements of courtesy and the inclination to
pursue her quarry as she addressed me, gazed surreptitiously
across the room where Lord Cathcart was chatting with an
animated Ferdy Courlan.

"It is always unwise to try to distract a gentleman when he
is discussing horseflesh. And from Mr. Courlan's apparent
enthusiasm, that must be the topic of discussion," I offered
sotto voce.

Miss Sandforth flushed, bit her lip, and deposited herself
on the sofa beside me.

"Oh Lady Constance!" She exclaimed. "You cannot possibly understand! You are beautiful and you know just what
to do and say in any situation, and I am certain that your
Mama never kept a list of eligibles whose attention you were

supposed to attract. And anyway, you are engaged now! You cannot know the worries that I live with!"

Miss Sandforth's agitation threatened her elaborate hairdo, as she emphasized her words with nods and shakes of her head.

Althea Sandforth was not among the new young ladies I had judged to be admirable—her voice was strident, her attitude petulant, her demeanor pushy, and her style in wardrobe and grooming more designed to show off the size of her dowry than enhance her admittedly meager attributes. But I understood her plight and sympathized with it more than she could have guessed.

"Surely, your mama does not expect you to attach Lord Cathcart."

I patted her hand to reassure her and to stop her shredding a perfectly good handkerchief.

"His determination to remain single is an established fact. More than that, there must be any number of gentlemen whose disposition is less daunting."

Miss Sandforth chewed on her lip thoughtfully for a moment. Her mama would have been better advised to concentrate on polishing her daughter's decorum than to encourage her to pursue an unattainable prize on the Marriage Mart.

"*You* did not look at all daunted just now, when Lord Cathcart was talking with *you*," she protested. "I am certain if I could only have a real opportunity to gain his attention, he would find I am not just the ordinary fresh-from-school miss."

No, indeed, Miss Sandforth was not an ordinary fresh-from-school miss. She had revealed herself to be astoundingly presumptuous, and foolish beyond imagination. I decided that my briefly felt sympathy for her was wasted. The calculation in her hazel eyes and pointed features was quite unbecoming.

"Are you going to the Fanshawe Ball, Lady Constance?"

I affirmed my intention to go.

"And Lord Cathcart is certain to be there too. After all, a

masked ball is so much more exciting than just an ordinary ball. I wonder what his disguise will be? Not that any costume could really disguise him."

The temptation was almost overwhelming. I owed neither Lord Cathcart nor Miss Sandforth a thing, and both had irritated me on what had otherwise been a quite satisfactory morning. But I resisted the impulse to tell her what she obviously was asking.

"I am an engaged lady, Miss Sandforth. Lord Cathcart would have no reason for disclosing his costume to me," I lied once more.

Miss Sandforth soon flounced off—no doubt to find someone more helpful to her ambitions.

After the guests left, I continued to think about the Fanshawe Ball. The matter of a costume needed to be decided as soon as possible. Considering my encounter with Lord Cathcart, I was inclined to find something as opposite to Cleopatra as I could discover.

"I am thinking of going as a nun," I told Drusilla as we sipped tea in my sitting room later that day. Medora, seated beside Drusilla, seemed to be pleased with both the almond biscuits and the lemon tarts that Cook had sent up.

"A nun!" Drusilla's golden eyes opened wide in astonishment.

I stirred my tea, trying to decide whether or not to discuss my extraordinary conversation with Lord Cathcart. But my friend spoke, resolving my dilemma.

"A nun," Drusilla repeated thoughtfully. "If you are not absolutely set on it, I might consider it for myself. Great Aunt Louisa is close to relenting and giving her permission for me to go." Drusilla laughed in her musical contralto. "I could not follow his line of reasoning exactly, but your Major Howells took it upon himself to convince my great aunt that for some reason, the preservation of propriety among the fashionable world depends upon my ameliorating influence at the Fanshawe Ball. My going as a nun might just prove to be the telling argument!"

I was so delighted that Major Howells had capably discharged his mission, I decided to be generous and let Drusilla use my idea for a disguise. But that still left me without one that would stand in stark contrast to Cleopatra.

"I have it!" Drusilla declared, looking very pleased. "You can go as Medora!"

"A little white dog?" I looked uncertainly at the creature who was licking a bit of lemon custard off her nose.

"Oh, Constance! For being the brightest and wittiest of ladies, you can be a bit slow sometimes! Not *that* Medora! *The* Medora!"

"You mean, dress in filmy scarves and those blousy harem trousers and wear a veil over the bottom half of my face?"

"Yes!" Drusilla affirmed with enthusiasm. "And you will probably need a dark wig, and that dark substance around your eyes, what is it called . . ."

"Kohl," I answered. "I believe it is called kohl." Lord Cathcart would assume I had tried for Cleopatra and had gotten the idea a little bit wrong.

I pretended to ponder the matter, and said, "I do not much feel like dressing as someone associated with the scandalous Lord Byron. I want to go as someone with more dignity."

"Why not Queen Elizabeth?" Drusilla suggested.

"Why not, indeed! I think I should like being a redhead very well!"

And no one would confuse either the costume or character of the Virgin Queen with Cleopatra!

And so I was feeling considerable satisfaction as I entered the dining room that evening. For some extraordinary reason, Mama, Papa, Jack and I were all at home and dined *en famille*.

"Constance, my love, was that Lord Cathcart I observed deep in conversation with you today?" No one could accuse Mama of being indirect.

"Yes, Mama. I believe that he was seeking refuge from Althea Sandforth's pursuit."

At least I was being partially truthful.

"That silly child! But what can one expect with such a foolish mother? If they are not both careful, they are going to waste the largest dowry to be available for as many years as I can remember. Certainly Alice Sandforth should know that Lord Cathcart is not in need of funds and is not likely to be drawn to a conniving miss with nothing else to recommend her!"

"I doubt that Mrs. Sandforth's assessment of her daughter's charms is as modest as yours, Mama," Jack offered with a smile.

"She has not been pursuing *you* has she, Jack?" Mama asked in horror.

"You have nothing to fear, Mama," Jack said reassuringly. "Miss Sandforth has much higher ambitions than a third son."

"Third son indeed! You are far above her expectations! The girl has no style, no grace! She would be fortunate beyond belief to attract your notice!"

Although sometimes Mama can be lacking in consistency, she is never lacking in loyalty. But perseverance is also one of her virtues, and she was not to be distracted from her discussion of Lord Cathcart.

"Constance, dear, how clever of you to attract Cathcart. His interest cannot but add to your aura of sophistication, and in a soon-to-be married lady, that is all to the good."

"Cathcart, you say?" Papa's baritone sounded from the head of the table, reminding us of his presence. "I cannot be easy about that. Constance, you are not to encourage his interest!"

"Julian! Surely you are not so removed from the social whirl that you do not remember how confirmed bachelors are want to seek out the company of engaged ladies? It is quite harmless, you know," Mama remonstrated.

"Harmless!" Papa harrumphed. "Cathcart has not been harmless since he was breeched! And there was that matter in Vienna . . . Constance, my dear, I mean what I say."

Since I had already decided to avoid Lord Cathcart if at

all possible, I had no problem nodding and looking dutiful. But I did want to know about "that matter in Vienna."

"Vienna . . . was Cathcart there . . ." Jack began.

"I am certain that your mother and sister do not wish to be bored with a discussion of Lord Cathcart's travels, Jack," Papa pronounced.

Of course that was total nonsense. One could almost see Mama planning to extract the entire story from Papa as soon as she was alone with him. And I, of course, was beside myself with frustrated curiosity. When had Lord Cathcart been in Vienna? What had he done there? I knew he and Papa were on speaking terms, or Mama would not have welcomed him as a guest during visiting hours. So probably "the matter" did not involve either treason or cheating at cards. But that left all sorts of other possibilities.

How I missed Prim! She was unrivalled as a discoverer of information from other servants. She would have had the full story within twelve hours.

Daisy was a dear, sweet, but oh so naïve! Worse yet, she was becoming increasingly absentminded, and I suspected none other than M. Armand was to blame. If she asked me once, she asked me four times a day when Lord Rochmont would return. If I answered her in matter-of-fact tones, she commented on my bravery while enduring a painful separation. If I displayed any impatience with her queries, she apologized for reminding me of my loneliness. I was quite certain that she was actually reflecting her own emotional state. So much for "out of sight, out of mind".

Jack was my only possible source of information regarding Lord Cathcart's behavior in Vienna. I resolved to interrogate him at the earliest possible moment.

Feeling rather at loose ends, I found my way to the library. I had finished my latest selections from Hookam's, and thought perhaps a volume of history would help put me to sleep later. As I was searching for just the right book, the aroma of cigars reached me and I saw that the door to the garden was ajar. Papa and Jack were smoking their post dinner cigars and sipping brandy in the garden. My pulse quickened. They might just be chatting about what Lord Cathcart had done in Vienna. So instead of honoring their privacy by leaving the room or closing the door, I tiptoed over to the door and strained to hear their conversation. But I soon discovered that I could catch only snatches, because as they smoked and chatted, they walked back and forth down a path that led from the library to a bench under an ancient oak that sheltered the northwest corner of the garden. I held my breath, praying they would not choose to come in or sit on the bench, which would put them beyond my range of hearing.

Papa seemed to be doing most of the talking with Jack just agreeing and asking the occasional question.

". . . damned fool Bourbons! After all the good English bloodshed to get their throne back . . ."

I had never heard Papa speak with such heat. He always seemed so calm and reasonable. His voice faded as they turned back toward the oak tree.

". . . Louis is not the problem. Must be the only one with half a brain. But that brother . . ."

Once more Papa's voice faded.

". . . appreciate your willingness to help."

Jack laughed. "Well, sir, I shall have certain compensation . . ."

I had forgotten all about Lord Cathcart and Vienna. Jack was involved in some special task for Papa. I longed to know what it was and I knew better than to come right out and ask. So I stayed by the door, waiting for them to return to hearing range.

". . . could upset, even destroy everything we have handed them. D'Artois must be rendered harmless, or . . . I say! My brandy could stand some freshening!"

I waited to hear no more. The brandy decanter was on a table not three feet away from me. I was relieved to make good my escape from the library, but I was frustrated by what I had overheard. Or more to the point, what I had not been able to overhear.

Fortunately, I had the matter of my costume for the Fanshawe Ball to distract me. The more I thought about it, the more pleased I was with the prospect of dressing as Queen Elizabeth. My height was a natural advantage, and given her love of adornment, I would have the opportunity to wear most of the contents of my jewel box. I considered the possibility of dying my hair with a henna rinse in order to avoid the nuisance of a wig. I was torn. Being a redhead for one night is one thing, committing oneself to it for the remainder of the season is quite another.

An Elizabethan gown presented few problems. The attics of Hatton House contained trunk loads of clothing from previous generations, and while none dated to the time in question, there were gowns from my grandmothers' time, which with slight alterations and the addition of a ruff, could be transformed into a convincing sixteenth century costume.

Daisy was enchanted by the idea, and I must admit that her sewing skills are some compensation for her lack in the area of information gathering. Happily the project of turning me out as a convincing monarch seemed to snap her out of the dream-like state in which she had been moving.

I impressed upon her the need for absolute secrecy. Her promises were heartfelt. My only fear was that her repeated declarations of her security measures might tempt the curiosity of staff, who ordinarily could care less about what I might be wearing to the Fanshawe Ball.

Drusilla's prediction that her choice of a nun's costume would sway her Great Aunt Louisa proved to be correct. That crusty lady did grant my friend permission to attend the ball.

But the matter of Lord Cathcart and Vienna continued to nag, and I was quite pleased when, two mornings after our family dinner, I encountered Jack alone in the breakfast room. I waited until he was on his second plate of ham, before beginning my inquiry with what I considered an indirect approach.

"I must say I was a bit surprised that Papa voiced concern

about a casual conversation I had with Lord Cathcart," I offered as an opening gambit.

"What a thing to say, Connie," Jack protested. "Papa might sometimes appear to be lost in his own interests, but he has never lacked in concern for any of his children."

"I do believe that you are deliberately misunderstanding me," I protested. There went subtlety and indirection. "I was referring to his concern about Lord Cathcart, not his concern about me! I have never before heard Papa say a critical word about Lord Cathcart. Indeed, it always seemed that they were on rather cordial terms."

Jack purposely bit into a muffin, which prevented him from answering. Was he learning evasive techniques at the Foreign Office?

I decided to drop all pretense of casual curiosity. It was not getting me anywhere.

"Do you know what I suspect, Jack?"

"Hmm," Jack replied around a bite of ham.

"I suspect that something happened in Vienna, just as you started to suggest. What happened? Was it during the Congress? What do you know? And do not dare take another bite before you answer me!"

Jack deliberately took a swallow of ale before responding.

"I really do not understand why you have any interest in the dull goings-on during the negotiations in Vienna."

"Dull goings-on indeed! I am not so sheltered to be ignorant of the fact that there were more than a few social scandals surrounding the official meetings. And I am convinced that Lord Cathcart was party to one. Please, Jack! Tell me what you know, or have heard!"

Jack shifted slightly in his chair and tapped a spoon on the table. "Really, Connie, I would not bother my pretty head about such matters if I were you."

I almost choked with rage. How dare my brother try to fob me off!

"John William Hatton, if you think for an instant that I

will accept such a tired and shabby dismissal, you have quite forgotten just how tenacious I can be!"

"Spare me, Connie, my memory in that department is fresh and is renewed routinely," Jack smiled wryly. "But I honestly do not understand your interest in Cathcart."

Jack suddenly sat up straight, put down the spoon he had been toying with, and fixed me with a stern glare.

"Are you contemplating a flirtation with him? For if you are, Connie, my girl, it would be worse than featherbrained on your part. Involvement with Cathcart would be foolhardy in the extreme."

I had decided to confide in no one about the interesting conversation I had had with Lord Cathcart, but before I knew what I was saying, I was telling Jack about Cathcart's reference to Rochmont's extended absence and about his suggestion that I complement his disguise at the Fanshawe Ball.

As I spoke, my usually carefree brother became grave. After I finished telling my story, he returned to his interest in his spoon, studying it intently and turning it over and back again. Then he looked up at me, concern showing clearly on his face.

"Honestly, Connie, I do not know what went on in Vienna. I think some countess was involved. It is not that Cathcart is dishonorable. But he does have the reputation for being devious. And somewhere I have come across rumors that he and your intended are not the best of friends—perhaps because of the countess. I would tread very carefully, if I were you."

That was certainly my intention. How else can one tread in the dark?

Chapter Eight

On the evening of the Fanshawe Ball, Drusilla Fortesque came early to Hatton House. While her great aunt had relented and given her permission for Drusilla to attend, no power on earth would have persuaded Louisa Fortesque to put in an appearance herself. So Mama, who would have risen from a sickbed for the Fanshawe Ball, agreed to serve as Drusilla's chaperone.

Drusilla knocked on the door of my dressing room as Daisy was transforming me into England's greatest monarch.

"Lands!" Daisy cried as Drusilla entered the dressing room. "You sure that's how a nun's s'posed to look, Miss Fortesque?"

"I hope not, Daisy," Drusilla laughed.

Who would have guessed that a severe ensemble of stark black and white could be so flattering? The flowing black robe skimmed Drusilla's generous curves and made her look svelte. The white of the wimple and coif set off her flawless, creamy-peach complexion, and drew attention to her finely arched brows, golden-brown eyes, and full, wide mouth, a mouth that would appear even more prominent when she was masked. Drusilla sparkled with excitement.

"I'll help you with your mask, Miss Fortesque, soon as I get this wig fixed on Lady Constance," Daisy offered.

Drusilla thanked her and pulled up a chair to watch me become redhaired.

Daisy dampened my hair and pinned it tightly to my head before carefully putting the wig in place. A single guinea gold curl peeped out, which she tucked out of sight. *A single guinea gold curl.* I wonder if either Drusilla or Daisy noticed the flush that spread over my face as I thought those words. Rochmont's harsh, enigmatic face rose unbidden in my mind's eye. Where was he? When would he return? What in heaven's name would I do when he did? At least I did not have to solve that problem this evening.

I stood and turned slowly so that Daisy could examine her handiwork and make any necessary adjustments. Then after Drusilla and I donned our masks, hers was black, mine, deepest green to match my velvet gown, we were pronounced dazzling by the ever enthusiastic Daisy.

Mama, Jack, and Major Howells were waiting for us at the foot of the stairs. Of course it was beneath Mama's dignity to go in full costume, but she joined in the spirit of disguise by wielding an elaborate mask on a stick. Decorated with feathers and sparkles to match the feathers and sparkles on her turban, its use was more to emphasize her sentences than to hide her identity. Not that anyone in the *ton* would mistake Mama for anyone else.

Major Howells was almost dashing dressed as a highwayman from the past century. His ensemble included shiny black boots, a sweeping black cape, and a brace of pistols, presumably unloaded.

But it was Jack who commanded attention. He was attired as the perfect Byronic hero, The Corsair, complete with a shirt exposing more chest than Louisa Fortesque would have approved, a scarf tying his inconveniently blond hair out of sight, an eye patch which almost made his mask redundant, and the apparently requisite brace of pistols along with a nasty looking scimitar.

I preceded Drusilla down the staircase, so it was not until after he had bowed over my hand that Major Howells experienced the full impact of Drusilla's appearance. I was pleased to note the familiar flush suffuse his face as he puzzled over the disparity between Drusilla's assumed identity as a nun, and the reality of her appearance.

"Miss Fortesque, what a stunning nun you make," he offered in amazement, as he greeted her.

Jack gave her a wicked grin. "On your way to confession, Sister?" he inquired.

"Not until tomorrow, Captain Hatton," Drusilla retorted.

Major Howells blinked in reaction to their exchange.

Mama, ever ready to avoid social awkwardness, suggested it was time for us to depart.

Since Mama never arrived at any ball a second before what, in her exacting calculations, was fashionably late, the masquerade was already in progress when we arrived. I suppose there were among the attendants some whose identity remained a mystery until the moment of unmasking at midnight, but most were quickly if not instantly identifiable. Who, for example could fail to recognize the galumphing Roman senator as Lord Bamwell? One more glass of punch and he was sure to trip on his toga! And the Cavalier with flowing curls and love knots who came to me to request the unmasking waltz was obviously Ferdy Courlan. No other gentleman of my acquaintance could have made such an embarrassing muddle of an invitation to dance.

"I say, Lady Constance, you make a truly lovely Virgin Queen . . . er . . . that is to say . . . that is what I hear she was called, don'tcha know . . ." Scarlet-faced, he continued. "Would count it a distinct honor if you would save that waltz for me when everyone reveals who he is . . . not that everyone doesn't already know . . . oh, did I spoil the game? Thousand pardons, I mean I thought you were Lady Constance, but your disguise is so complete, I can't be sure, don'tcha know."

Ferdy swallowed and swept from his face some curls that were threatening to obscure his vision, before manfully trying to complete his mission. Of course, I could have put him out of his misery by simply saying, "Yes, thank you, Mr. Courlan", but I was momentarily transfixed by his ramblings.

"It is just that you are betrothed, Lady Constance, and the . . . uh . . . object, so to speak of your betrothal . . . being absent . . ."

I repressed a sigh. If Ferdy Courlan was aware of Rochmont's extended absence, it could only be because it had become a subject of the betting books at Whites. I refrained from asking him the exact nature of his own bet on just how long the odds were that Rochmont would return before the end of the season.

"I thought," he continued, describing his mental processes generously, "that it might be easier for both of us, I, being unattached and with no designs on your person, don't-cha know, and you being temporarily *unattached*, so to speak . . ." At which point, he lost track of his sentence and took a deep breath before trying to discover just where he had left it. The time had come for me to be gracious.

"Why Mr. Courlan! How terribly thoughtful of you to rescue me from either being abandoned or having to repel unwelcome attentions at the romantic apex of the evening! Of course, I shall be delighted to save the unmasking waltz for you!"

He managed a "my pleasure" and a quick bow, which slightly dislodged his enormous wig, tipping it rakishly over his left eyebrow.

I spied two Cleopatras. One, whose childlike whispers and elegant figure confirmed her to be Lady Antony, was the partner of a Roman soldier—perhaps Alastair Plinkin-don. I made a mental note to discover if Jack or Lady Antony had been the first to back away from their budding romance.

The second Cleopatra was none other than Althea Sand-forth, who could be seen scanning the crowd for better prospects as she danced with a Scottish chieftain I was certain was Freddie Stanhope.

My attention was diverted as a creature dressed as Medora floated into the ballroom. She was attired exactly as I had pictured the Corsair's lover should be dressed: gauzy shirt and full, flowing trousers, embroidered slippers turning up at the toes, a straight black wig with fringe, and a transparent veil covering the lower half of her face. The veil did not obscure the beauty mark by the lady's mouth. And above the veil, a pair of caramel-colored eyes regarded my brother Jack with something warmer than a polite welcome. There was an audible rise in the volume of chatter as they became the focus of every eye in the ballroom. Jack and Lady Norham! What could my charming brother be thinking? Perhaps I did not want to know.

It was a relief when Major Howells appeared for his promised dance, and the evening and I moved along from dance to dance, partner to partner, until a dance that I had purposely reserved for a fictitious partner arrived and I began to move toward the ladies' retiring room for some much needed rest and the chance to hear what the gossips were saying.

But before I could make good my escape, an Elizabethan gentleman approached me. I might have recognized him anyway, but his bored, silky voice and the bits of silver glittering in the slits of his black mask made his identity certain.

I consciously braced myself for the encounter. The slight upward turn of his mouth told me he detected my discomfort. I decided to play my assumed role so that as an Elizabethan gentleman, he would need to respond as my subject. If I had to deal with Lord Cathcart, monarch to subject was the relationship to assume.

I extended my hand with regal condescension.

"Sir Walter Raleigh, my dutiful servant, I presume."

Lord Cathcart swept a bow, took my hand in both of his, and kissed it lingeringly. I am sure my face matched my hair.

"Bess, my darling, Queen of My Heart. Surely you recognize your own dearest Robin!" His lips returned to my hand. He had neatly checkmated my roleplaying gambit.

"A romance between Leicester and Queen Elizabeth has never been proven, my lord, and I consider your behavior to border on *lese majeste!*"

Lord Cathcart slowly released my hand and assumed a challenging stance, right hand resting on his dress sword, which looked as if it might very well be capable of deadly work.

"At least, Robert Dudley survived the good queen's interest with his head on his shoulders. Old Raleigh donated his cloak and lost his head as a way of thanks. Too high a price for chivalry, I think."

"Such lack of devotion!" I protested haughtily.

Before I knew what was happening, Lord Cathcart had moved to my side, and taking my arm in a firm grip, began to steer me toward a draped alcove at the edge of the dance floor.

"One must indeed sympathize with the lack of devotion you are suffering," he murmured. "Or is Rochmont sending you daily *billets* swearing his undying love?"

"My relationship with Lord Rochmont is none of your affair," I responded testily, dropping all pretense of playing the role of imperious queen.

"How flattered I am that you should show an interest in my affairs, Lady Constance."

Lord Cathcart paused and once more lifted my hand for a languid kiss.

I glanced about furtively, but partygoers appeared to be sufficiently engrossed that I saw no one observing Lord Cathcart and me. This time, I did not wait for him to release my hand, but snatched it back in a decidedly non-regal manner.

"You will cease this undue familiarity at once, my lord!" I hissed.

"Or you will—what—Lady Constance? Claw my cheek, leaving five fresh rivulets of blood? Administer a resounding slap across my insolent visage, leaving the imprint of your dainty hand for all to see? Snatch my sword, tearing my shirt before I can wrest the weapon from your trembling hand? Which scene do you wish to play out for the entertainment of the ballgoers and the enlightenment of your neglectful fiancé?"

Lord Cathcart was uncomfortably close to me in the dark, confined space of the alcove. The faint scent of sandalwood tickled my nose. He had positioned himself directly in front of the meeting of the draperies, blocking most of the available light and also my escape.

He laughed softly, and gripped my arms. I could not see his face clearly, but as he spoke, his breath ruffled the red curls of my wig.

"Ah, Constance, my dear. I am not at all sure I would object to any of the scenes I suggested. But I do believe I prefer the scene that requires you to tear off my shirt. I cannot think it would be objectionable at all to be in a cozy spot with you, *sans* shirt."

His insinuating laugh made me feel chilled in spite of the warm night and confined space. As he bent with the obvious intention of kissing me, I stepped firmly on his foot, eliciting a groan of pain.

He released me, but remained planted firmly in front of my only exit. When he spoke, his voice was icy, which, curiously cured my chill.

"So that is the way it is, my dear. You silly, silly little girl, letting yourself fall under Rochmont's spell."

"Just because I resist your very unwelcome advances does not mean I am under Lord Rochmont's or anybody else's spell," I protested.

"For your sake, I hope that declaration is truer than it sounds. I could tell you some stories about your absent fiancé." Cathcart's voice was soft and slightly menacing.

"I do not care . . ." I began, but Lord Cathcart interrupted me.

"You do not care to know the truth about Rochmont, because you care for him, is that not so, Lady Constance? But I shall tell you at least one truth about the man whose spell you seem to be under. I shall tell you where he is, where he has been this past week or more. Paris. He is in Paris. And do you know why I am certain that he is in Paris?"

I wanted to put my hands over my ears and scream to

drown out Lord Cathcart's voice. No! No! No! I did not want
to know why Lord Cathcart was so certain that Rochmont
was in Paris. But I remained where I was, bracing myself for
the blow that I knew was coming, grateful that the light in
the alcove was too dark to reveal either a blush or blanche.

"I am certain Rochmont is in Paris because the enchant-
ing Countess Magda is in Paris!"

There was gloating in Cathcart's pronouncement. He
swept me a low bow, and departed the alcove.

I stood alone in the darkness trying to slow my hammer-
ing heart, calm my jangled nerves, and sort out my confused
thoughts. Why had Cathcart made romantic advances?
Clearly, he had no genuine affection, much less love for me.
I doubted he was capable of such tender feelings. But he certainly was capable of anger and resentment—and revenge.
He took no pains to hide his dislike of Rochmont. Papa's order for me to avoid Lord Cathcart echoed in my brain. The
rumors Jack had heard about Vienna must be true. I suspected that Lord Cathcart wished to use me to settle a score
with my absent fiancé. A rivalry involving a beautiful countess named Magda, no doubt.

I felt a childish urge to stay in the darkened alcove for the
rest of the ball. But doing so would risk the gossip and potential scandal that I had so narrowly avoided. I blinked
away threatening tears, took a deep breath, and squared my
shoulders. All I had to do was maintain my composure for
the remainder of the ball, and then I could retire to the safety
of my own room and Daisy's coddling. Perhaps I would suc-
cumb to a brief illness—a fever, or a chill?

I consoled myself in the knowledge that at least I was
helping Drusilla to have a happier future than she could have
expected without my good offices. I noticed that Major
Howells had taken her into supper, almost a declaration of
serious intentions. I returned resolutely to the ballroom for
the country dance I had promised Alastair Plinkindon.

Our set included Drusilla and Major Howells, Ferdy
Courlan and Lady Antony, along with Jack and Althea

Sandforth. We were still officially anonymous behind our masks, but actually, fully aware of each one's identity. We were an odd lot. Miss Sandforth did not seem to be able to decide whether to flirt with Jack, or scan the ballroom to discover the whereabouts of Lord Cathcart. I could have told her not to waste her eyesight looking for him on the dance floor. Lord Cathcart danced only waltzes and the occasional quadrille. A country dance was beneath his dignity.

Jack divided his time between encouraging Miss Sandforth to greater and greater indiscretion in her flirtation, smiling reassuringly at Lady Antony, and, when the dance pattern brought them together, whispering asides to Drusilla that were making her blush.

Beneath his rakish mask, Major Howells' jaw was rigidly set, as if he were guarding words he preferred not to utter. Mr. Plinkindon and I, each for personal reasons, were engaged in a most determinedly lighthearted conversation about nothing at all. For her part, Lady Antony somehow maintained her usual cool grace in spite of the fact that her partner, Ferdy Courlan provided distraction for the rest of us, by repeatedly forgetting the steps and ending up in the wrong place with the wrong partner, or no partner at all.

As the orchestra played the final bars of the dance, and all in our set were sighing in relief, poor Ferdy miscued once more, backing Lady Antony into a potted orange tree at the edge of the dance floor. The unmistakable sound of ripping fabric could be heard over the fading notes of the music.

Lady Antony's lovely face was a study in horror as she realized that her Cleopatra costume, never substantial to begin with, had torn, neck to hem.

But even before Althea Sandforth could summon a deep breath for a shriek that would announce Lady Antony's plight to the entire ballroom and possibly make her the *on dit* of the evening, Major Howells swept off his highwayman's black cape and wrapped it about Lady Antony's shoulders.

The good major did not blush at all when Lady Antony turned her ineffably tender violet eyes up to him and, in her softest of childlike tones thanked him for valor worthy of a Knight of the Round Table. But the impact of this accolade caused Major Howells to forget all rules of gentlemanly behavior, and he departed the dance floor, not with his partner, Drusilla Fortesque, but with Lady Antony, supporting her with an arm around her shoulder and asking if she perhaps needed some medicinal brandy.

Ferdy Courlan, never the quickest witted, could not be counted upon to step into the breach created by the departure of Major Howells and Lady Antony. He was still trying to make sense of what had happened.

"Er . . . I say . . . awfully sorry . . . didn't see that plant there before. Suppose it could have grown in the heat of the room? Is deucedly hot in here . . ."

Before I could think of a way to rescue Drusilla from the embarrassment of leaving the dance unattended, she announced that her wimple had come loose during the exertions of the dance, and asked me to accompany her to repair it.

In the ladies' retiring room, Drusilla made no attempt to adjust her wimple, but collapsed on a slipper chair. She was fanning herself languidly and half laughing, half chuckling in her uniquely throaty tone.

"Ferdy Courlan is a prize, is he not? I vow, if it did not require that I spend the entire balance of my earthly life with him, I would be tempted to trick him into a compromising situation so he would be forced to propose marriage. One would be guaranteed continual amusement in his company! But I suppose, after a few years of his bumbling contretemps, one would become irritated rather than amused."

"How could you even consider Ferdy when there is someone like Major Howells!" I protested. "Although, I must say, I was astonished that he left you stranded at the end of the country dance. Even with all the commotion over Lady Antony's dress, one would expect him to have the presence of mind to escort you from the dance floor as he ought to have!"

"Oh, I would not be at all surprised if I am something of a

disappointment to the very proper Major Howells," my friend said matter of factly.

I could not believe my ears, or my eyes, as I watched her continuing to fan herself as if nothing in the world were amiss.

"But surely that is not true!" I exclaimed.

My own future might be spinning beyond my control in a most distressing way, but I could not countenance the perfect destiny I had devised for Drusilla Fortesque being frustrated too!

"You must not refine too much upon his leaving the dance floor with Lady Antony, you know. When she turns those pansy eyes on any gentleman, they all seem to forget good common sense—even a very sensible gentleman such as Major Howells," I added, putting his negligence in the best light I could.

At last, Drusilla stopped fanning and looked directly at me. Well that was an improvement! We would never get her future settled without a little concentration on her part.

"Oh, *that*! *That* was not what I was referring to! But I do agree Lady Antony's gaze is mesmerizing to all gentlemen. No, I believe Major Howells became disenchanted with me during supper."

She tapped her closed fan on her chin.

I was diverted for a moment by the idea of a nun carrying a fan, but I called my attention back to the problem of Drusilla's relationship with Major Howells. I could not let myself be sidetracked into thinking about such irrelevancies as nuns and fans when Drusilla's future was at stake.

"How could you have possibly disenchanted him at supper!" I refused to consider such an idea. "Your table manners are flawless!"

Drusilla chuckled. How could she find anything amusing in the situation?

"Constance, my dear, I am grateful for your confidence in me! No, I did not drink from my finger bowl, nor smear butter on my wine glass. But I am afraid the conversation drifted toward poetry. That is shocking enough. I should have had the self-discipline not to indulge in a topic so open to avenues where ladies do not tread. But in my defense, I must say your brother egged me on."

She smiled wryly, shrugged, and resumed fanning.

"I fear I delivered myself of an unvarnished opinion about the unrealistic idealism of much of current poetry. I thought poor Major Howells would choke on a lobster patty! I do not know which shocked him most, my opinion, the fact that I expressed an opinion, or the fact that I had an opinion to express."

She chuckled again, remembering the scene.

I, on the other hand, could barely suppress tears. It had been a thoroughly trying evening. My own future looked grim, regardless of how my engagement to Rochmont was resolved. My brother showed every appearance of being enthralled by Lady Norham, who was no lady. I had made an enemy of the most ruthless man in the *ton*, and my thoughtful planning for the happiness of my friend was in danger of coming to naught.

Drusilla's laughter stopped abruptly.

"Oh, Constance, I am so very sorry!"

She sounded genuinely contrite. Perhaps the situation was not beyond mending.

"You cannot imagine how deeply grateful I am for your friendship and for your selfless concern for my happiness. But really and truly, Constance, darling, Major Howells and I would make a perfectly miserable pair, you know."

I knew nothing of the sort. And I am sure my shock at her words showed clearly on my face.

"How can you say such a thing, Drusilla! You would be a *perfect* match!"

"Whatever makes your think so?" she inquired. "The fact that I *look* dull and the fact that he *is* dull?"

She had scarcely spoken the words when she flushed and bit her lower lip.

"I do apologize, Constance! What a perfectly dreadful thing to think, much less say! And so unfair to Major Howells!"

She shrugged and shook her head. "Well, there you have it in a nutshell, why the worthy Major and I would not suit. I cannot seem to control my unruly thoughts or my unruly tongue. I would impose embarrassment after embarrassment on him, just as I did at supper tonight!"

My disappointment was too keen for me to immediately acknowledge the sense of what she said.

"But the two of you seemed so well suited," I protested weakly.

"Constance, Constance," Drusilla shook her head and patted my hand in the manner of a kindly older sister.

"Be honest. Major Howells and I appeared to be a convenient match because we are both slight anomalies in the *ton*. I come from a respectable family, but I am too old for a first season. I am neither an heiress nor destitute. I am of no interest to the fashionable world. Major Howells is of more interest because he is an eligible man with a fortune. But it is obvious that he will never care to learn the niceties of fashionable repartee. On the one hand, he has no patience for the prattle of young misses, and on the other, the flirtation of more sophisticated, worldly-wise ladies makes him observably uncomfortable."

"That is precisely why . . ." I began.

"Yes, I know," Drusilla patted my hand again in her older sister manner. "I know that is what you understood, and why you have been so eager to help me make a match with Major Howells. And I concede that, at first glance, we appear to be a quite likely couple. But Major Howells has the advantage of being what he appears to be—a solid, conservative gentleman of military background. Unfortunately, I am not what I appear to be—comfortably dowdy."

I started to protest my friend's description of herself, but she silenced me with another pat on my hand.

"Save your breath to cool your porridge, Constance. I have a looking glass. And I also know I will never have sufficient patience to do what needs to be done to 'make the most of my assets', as Great Aunt Louisa is constantly advising. But even if I did expend more energy on my appearance, I would still not be a comfortable match for someone like Major Howells. The real problem is my unruly thoughts, and my unfortunate habit of speaking them at just the wrong moment, as I did at supper tonight.

"Oh, I suppose that if I truly cared for Major Howells, I could teach myself greater discipline. But thus far, I have never had the motivation to please anyone but myself! Major Howells deserves better in a wife. And I do believe that if he insists upon it, he will get it!"

I wondered briefly what happens if one does care sufficiently for someone to alter one's behavior—and the other one does not notice—or does not care. But I would not let myself dwell on such a depressing thought.

"Oh dear, Drusilla," I said wearily as I checked my reflection before returning to the rigors of the dance floor. "I do apologize if my playing matchmaker for you and Major Howells has caused you embarrassment."

"Nonsense!" was the reply of my determinedly common-sensical friend. "No harm was done, and it was rather pleasant to be regarded appraisingly by some of the mamas of young misses who are hopeful of attaching Major Howells' fortune, if not his affection."

I returned to the ballroom for my waltz with Ferdy Courlan, determined to learn some of my friend's cool common sense. Not that common sense alone would help me survive a waltz with Ferdy, who was eying the potted orange trees that lined the ballroom as he led me to the dance floor. He was still fretting over his accident with Lady Antony.

The strains of a particularly romantic waltz began, and Ferdy and I warily began to dance, keeping well away from the perimeter of the floor, which is why, at first, I was not aware that some dancers had stopped dancing. But the sudden silencing of all conversation did finally penetrate my brain, and I looked up at Ferdy's face to see him smiling as if his favorite horse had won a match race. And, in a sense it just might have. I turned to look where he and everyone else was looking.

Sauntering across the floor, making his way toward us was a gentleman of no more than average height dressed in black evening attire with sparkling white linen. He was wearing a black mask that in no way disguised the fact that he was none other than Blaise de Grenault, Lord Rochmont. As he came to where Ferdy and I were standing, a slight smile relieved the harsh planes of his face. He nodded to Ferdy.

"Thank you for saving my place," he said.

"A pleasure, Rochmont," Ferdy assured him. "If you will just excuse me, I believe I will toddle off to White's. Have a bit of a wager, don'tcha know."

And there, in front of everyone, my errant fiancé pulled me into a rather close embrace. Fortunately, the orchestra had not stopped playing, so when we began to dance, other dancers did too.

"You make a stunning redhead," Rochmont whispered in my ear.

I pulled myself as far back as his arms would allow and glared at him. Only the candlelight reflected in his eyes distinguished them from his mask.

"It is all right, Constance, he said soothingly. "No doubt you have been struggling to fight off the unwelcome attentions of half the gentlemen in London. But those problems are over."

I had no doubt that my problems had just multiplied.

"How dare you make such a public spectacle," I hissed.

"Forgive me, my dear," he said contritely. "I fear the joy of seeing you once more has impaired my good judgment. Of course you are right. Privacy is called for."

He relaxed his hold, and we danced—almost floated around the room, swaying, twirling, waltzing as no couple had ever before waltzed, whirling, right though the doors leading out of the lighted ballroom, onto the terrace overlooking a garden.

In a heartbeat, I was in his arms, being kissed on my forehead, my nose, my ears, my lips . . . It was just the occasion on which I should have sought to employ the sort of common sense I am sure Drusilla would have used. But I was concentrating all of my powers to remain standing on legs that had apparently turned to ribbons. The best I could do was hold on to Rochmont and try to remember to breathe, which was essential, because my heart was racing so rapidly. I wanted to speak some words of caution to him, but that was impossible to do. My mouth was otherwise occupied, and my brain was not functioning.

I felt a cooling breeze on my neck and the delicious sensation of Rochmont's lips warming the exact place the breeze had just cooled. *My neck! My ruff*! The shock brought me back to my senses.

"Stop instantly! My ruff is gone!"

"Hmm" was his reply, his chin nuzzling the top of my head. "It was in the way."

His chin was nuzzling the top of my head!

"My wig!" I cried.

"It was in the way too," he laughed. "So are these dratted hairpins."

I could hear the "ping, ping" of hairpins hitting the marble terrace.

"What am I to do?" I wailed.

"I thought you were doing very well indeed," was his reply. He was still laughing.

"You do not understand," I protested. "We could be discovered at any moment!"

"That is true," he agreed.

He stopped removing hairpins, and holding me in a loose embrace, looked at me directly.

"And just what do you think would happen if we are discovered?" He smiled his half smile. "We have already announced our betrothal. I daresay your parents might expect us to announce a wedding date."

My face must have reflected how stunned I was at such an idea, for he smiled and gently patted my cheek.

"I know, I know, I just now returned, and it is much too soon for you to think about that! I fear you have sustained something of a shock. When I arrived at the ball, I sent a note to your mother saying that I would be seeing you home. My carriage is waiting in the lane behind the garden."

As Rochmont guided me through the dimly lit garden filled with the murmurs of other couples, I realized he had orchestrated the entire sequence of our reunion. It had been out of my control even before he had sauntered across the ballroom to relieve poor Ferdy of the task of dancing with me.

I should have taken advantage of our journey to Hatton House to quiz him on where he had been over the past fortnight. I should have seized the opportunity to inquire if he was acquainted with a certain Countess Magda. I did neither. I did not say a word. Neither did Rochmont. He seemed to understand how utterly weary I was, so weary that resting my head on his shoulder all the way home was somehow comforting. He did kiss me as we parted. Not the sort of tempestuous kiss of the terrace, just a gentle brushing of his lips on mine and an equally gentle, "Good night, sweetheart. Pleasant dreams."

Chapter Nine

I suppose Perkins opened the door for me, but I could not swear to it. I ascended the staircase to my room oblivious of my surroundings, my head feeling as light as the bubbles in the champagne I had drunk. Many questions needed to be asked and answered. Had Rochmont really been in Paris during the whole of his absence? How well did he know Countess Magda? And, most importantly, did he have any fond feelings for me, Lady Constance Hatton? That was the most important question of all. But it was one question I would never stoop to ask. The melody of the waltz Rochmont and I had danced to played in my mind, and I hummed along as I made my way down the hallway.

Dim light shone beneath my bedroom door. I could count on Daisy to be there to help me undress, eager for a report on my evening. The very first thing I noticed when I opened the door was the prevailing fragrance of lilies of the valley. A glance revealed that vases of those delicate blossoms graced every available surface.

Next I noticed Daisy, sitting in her accustomed chair, smiling in her sleep, clutching a bouquet of daisies to her heart. Monsieur Armand had returned with his master.

As the door clicked shut, Daisy stirred and wakened, looking momentarily confused. She struggled to her feet, sending daisies over the floor.

"Lady Constance . . . oh dear! My marguerites!" She exclaimed in despair.

For a minute we were both engaged in retrieving the flowers, which showed wear from having been tightly clutched for an extended period of time. I removed the lilies of the valley from a vase and replaced them with Daisy's bouquet, which immediately showed signs of recovery.

"Oh, thank you, Lady Constance. I know I should'uv put them in water straight off, but I never had no bouquet before . . . I just wanted to hold them for a while . . . must have drifted off . . ." Daisy regarded the bouquet with a soft, unfocused smile.

"He came back, Lady Constance, Monsewer Armand. And he came to see me first thing and brung me my very first bouquet. Daisies because of my name. Only he said in French they're marguerites. What a fancy name! Never knowed that!"

"How thoughtful of him," I managed. Counseling caution at this hour was useless, and as well directed at myself as my maid.

"Oh, Lady Constance! What's happened to my brain?"

Probably turned to the same porridge as mine for a very similar reason, I thought silently.

"You must be the happiest lady in London! Lord Rochmont is back! He sent all of these flowers for you. Monsewer Armand brung them, too."

"Lord Rochmont came to the ball."

I refused to confirm that I was the happiest lady in London, but Daisy obviously did not notice my omission.

"Well, now, I'll just help you out of your gown and get you all tucked in for a nice long sleep, Lady Constance."

But as she began to unfasten my gown, she returned to reality sufficiently to notice certain missing items.

"Lady Constance! Your ruff! Your wig!"

But I also had returned sufficiently to reality to notice certain *other* missing items.

"Daisy!" I countered. "Your fichu! Your cap!"

She flushed crimson. I felt cruel.

"Never mind, Daisy. Perhaps you would be good enough to go to Fanshawe Place tomorrow and see if you can retrieve my ruff and wig. If they have not been found, ask to look on the terrace near the ballroom door. You might find some serviceable hairpins in the same location."

Daisy assumed her idea of a worldly-wise air. "Do not worry about it for a minute, Lady Constance. I shall be—what is Lord Chase always saying—the soul of discretion."

"And while you are being discreet, Daisy, try to replace your cap and fichu before Lady Chase sees you."

Cannot let servants get the upper hand, now, can we?

I am not going to report the substance of my dreams that night. Suffice it to say, the glow I felt when waking owed nothing to the sunlight streaming though my bedroom curtains.

When Daisy appeared, I noticed a reddening of certain areas of her pale face and neck. If the cause were apparent to me, it would also be apparent to every other resident of Hatton House. I silently thanked Heaven that the master had not been as eager as the servant—at least not too eager to neglect shaving before presenting himself. Answering inquiries about my fiancé's return was going to be difficult enough without having to face the world with visible evidence of the happy reunion. I mentally added this transgression to the Bill of Particulars against "Monsewer" Armand that I intended to take up with the responsible authority at the first possible occasion.

But Daisy showed no trace of embarrassment as she set a tray on my bedside table on which sat not only my cup of tea, but a bunch of white violets—where on earth could they have come from so late in the season—and a note addressed to Lady Constance Hatton in a firm masculine hand which matched exactly the writing on two other notes resting in the drawer of that very bedside table.

Daisy fairly floated about the room, oblivious of my impatience to read the note in privacy. She checked the water level in all ten vases of lilies of the valley, chattering as she did so.

"Monsewer Armand brung the note and them perty violets."

Here she paused and patted a small bunch of daisies pinned to the *v* of her fichu. M. Armand had brought more than just my note and violets.

"I'n't that funny though . . . never thought a that afore . . . white violets . . . violet means purple, dun't it?"

She stood still for a moment, vase in hand as she considered the problem. Then her face brightened as she thought of a possible solution.

"Oh, pr'haps that's just in English," she offered. "I'll wager the French have a different name for violets, a fancier name, just like with daisies and marguerites."

"It is fancier, Daisy, but it is essentially the same, *'violette'*."

Her face fell. She had, no doubt, hoped to impress "Monsewer" Armand with a new vocabulary word.

"I will probably need you to take an answer to Lord Rochmont's note shortly, Daisy, if you have the time."

This one perfect sentence not only restored Daisy's spirits, but also motivated her to finish her self-appointed tasks in my bedroom, giving me the privacy I was longing for. She left the room, humming softly to herself.

I wasted no time reading the note.

Dear Constance,

I trust you slept well. I hope that you will be able to spare me some of your time today. Perhaps a turn in the park before the fashionable hour would make conversation possible?

> *Seeing you once more reminds me forcibly how fortunate a man I am to be the betrothed of such a beautiful lady.*
>
> *Yours faithfully,*
> *Blaise*

"Yours faithfully"; was there any meaning to his chosen valediction? I reread and again reread the short missive, my heart pounding at the prospect of being alone with this cipher of a man. I dreaded to once more broach the subject of his servant's over-familiarity with Daisy. But he had promised to "have a talk" with Armand. Thus far, the content of said "talk" might have been lessons in seduction, if Daisy's behavior was any indication.

And perhaps, what the servant was doing, the master also intended. I felt a blush spreading from my bosom to hairline as I remembered my lack of the most basic decorum in his arms the night before. I felt as gullible as Daisy. At least it was possible that her "Monsewer" had spoken words of love or affection. Rochmont had never even hinted at any feelings stronger than admiration for my face, form and fashion sense. Was he even capable of the love and devotion I longed for? And, if so, would I be the object?

Lady Norham's mocking smile once more flashed in my mind. She and Jack had been too cozy with each other for my taste. For a second, I even considered the possibility that Jack might marry the woman! But I remembered her fortune hunting ways and purged from my mind the vision of enduring Lady Norham's condescension at years of family gatherings. Even if Jack might be selfish enough to inflict such a fate on me, I could rely upon Lady Norham's avarice to spare me.

I drank my now cool tea, and composed an answer to Rochmont's note.

> *Dear Rochmont,*
>   *Thank you for the delightful posies. Where on earth
> did you find such blossoms so late in the season?*
>   *Would half past three be convenient?*
>
>   *Sincerely,*
>   *Constance*

I reviewed it with some satisfaction, knowing that a more honest response would have read:

> *Dear Blaise,*
>   *Indeed, I did sleep well, dreaming blissful dreams
> that, perhaps, some day, I will be able to share with you.*
>   *Thank you for the lovely flowers. How clever of you
> to be able to find them so late in the season, and how
> clever of you to send blossoms with such a subtle but
> pervasive fragrance that the giver's identity is con-
> stantly brought to mind.*
>   *You speak of wishing to have private conversation
> with me. Is it really just conversation you had in mind?*
>   *Is your admiration for my person matched by any
> finer feelings? Have you truly been faithful during our
> separation?*
>
>   *Eagerly awaiting your response,*
>   *Connie*

That was a note best left unsent. Better still, unwritten.

I congratulated myself on my clear judgment, and set my mind to what I would wear for the outing to come. I pulled a pale peach muslin sprigged in light green from my wardrobe and was considering its merits when Daisy announced Miss Fortesque was downstairs inquiring if Medora might enjoy a walk.

"Ask her to come up, if she would, please, Daisy," I said, truly delighted for a diversion from my ruminations about the previous evening and just how I should best approach my afternoon drive.

"And, I think Medora might be found in the kitchen, if you would bring her up too," I added absently, contemplating the light green bonnet with peach ribbons, made to go with the peach muslin.

I set the gown on my bed along with the bonnet to make certain that the peach in the satin ribbons and muslin gown really did go as well together as they had seemed to when I had purchased them.

Upon close examination in the unforgiving sunlight, I felt reassured that in matters of fashion, at least, my judgment remained unimpaired.

Drusilla swept into the room, filling it with her generous cheerfulness.

"Oh, Constance! What a perfectly divine gown and bonnet! You cannot be thinking of wearing them just to take Medora for a walk!"

I smiled and kissed the air next to Drusilla's cheek.

"I suppose what I am wearing will do for walking Medora," I said, looking in the glass at my sky blue morning gown. "I was just deciding on something to wear this afternoon for a drive in the park."

"With Lord Rochmont!" Drusilla exclaimed, her eyes sparkling with excitement and questions.

"Yes," I confirmed, "with Lord Rochmont."

If my friend heard the ambivalence in my tone, she chose to ignore it.

"Constance! Never could I imagine a more dramatic or romantic scene than his return to you during the ball last night. And the way the two of you waltzed together! Honestly, Constance, no one could keep from watching! But at the same time, I felt that we were all—how can I put this? Intruding. That is what we were all doing. We were intruding on what should have been a very private moment. But I just could not refrain from watching, even though I wanted to tell everyone else to go about their own activities and let you and Lord Rochmont have some time to become reacquainted."

I could have assured her that we had, indeed, become most decidedly "reacquainted", but I refrained.

"So I was pleased to see that you escaped to the privacy of the terrace."

I should have known Drusilla would miss nothing. Afraid I might be blushing, I held the bonnet's ribbons against the gown, pretending to make the judgment I had already made.

But Drusilla saw my embarrassment.

"I am so dreadfully sorry, Constance for making such a personal allusion!" Drusilla exclaimed contritely. "I really did not mean to presume, honestly! But it could not have been easy for you these past few days, with Lord Rochmont gone, and tongues wagging the way they do! I thought he acted masterfully in scotching any gossip that perhaps he was not attached to you. No one present last night has the least doubt Lord Rochmont is delighted to be your betrothed."

I was too surprised to disguise my reaction. I dropped the bonnet without bothering to make sure it landed on the bed.

"You honestly believe that?" I asked searchingly, sacrificing pride in my need for reassurance.

Drusilla's bright smile faded as she studied my flushed face.

"Why Constance! Of course I am certain! So is everyone who was at the ball! There was not one lady in the room who would not have parted with every jewel in her collection to be the focus of the sort of attention Lord Rochmont paid you last night!"

A tiny frown clouded her face for a moment.

"Anyway, I had understood yours and Lord Rochmont's betrothal, while based on a certain element of mutual liking, was one of the more enlightened arrangements, arrived at by a clear understanding of each other's character and expectations."

Just how wide of the mark her assumption was must have been reflected in my face.

She sat down on a small sofa, seemingly unable to take

the weight of the implications of her misunderstanding. I sat beside her, weary with dissembling.

"Constance, dearest friend," she said gently, "I am so very dreadfully sorry for continuing to tread where angels would know better. Please forgive me! I see I have leapt to all sorts of unwarranted conclusions about you and Lord Rochmont. It is just that the two of you seemed so well suited! Such an exception to the matches that I see forming among other couples."

Drusilla gave a tiny shrug and looked the picture of contrition.

"Please do not apologize," I reassured her. "I cannot believe that I am fortunate enough to have a friend who is actually concerned about my best interests. And usually, I trust your judgment without question." I smiled ruefully.

"And I must admit," I added, "I am aching with curiosity to know how such a level-headed lady as you are came to the conclusion that Lord Rochmont and I are a nearly perfect match."

Drusilla settled back into the corner of the sofa and traced the outline of the design in the brocade covering its arm.

"Actually, I am terribly embarrassed to admit that I have made any assessment of what is a matter strictly between you and Lord Rochmont—and your families, of course."

"Nonsense, Drusilla, do not be tiresome! Other than shopping, dressing, and going to various entertainments, what does one do but make assessments of others' personal relationships!"

We both laughed. Drusilla relaxed, and stopped tracing the brocade design.

"Well, of course I have never met Lord Rochmont. Indeed, I had never seen him until last night. But from the minute he entered the ballroom, I knew precisely who he was. That was partly because he scarcely glanced across the room before he headed directly to you. But it was also because of his presence, his bearing. One hears of it whenever his name is mentioned. It is difficult to explain. One senses that here is a man who is not to be trifled with. One would think carefully before withholding information from a man like that. One does not fear him, but neither would one—or I, at least—want to cross him."

"Heavens, Drusilla! And here I just named you the best of friends!" I declared in only partially mock reproach. "What a fate you wish on me, marrying such a daunting individual!"

Drusilla studied me through narrowed eyes.

"And just what sort of man do you wish to marry, Constance? One that your father and brothers treat with courtesy because he is your husband, or one who can actually hold his own in their company?"

It was good I was sitting down, for my world tilted just a bit at her words. My friend had, in one sentence, distilled the reason why I had played the game that had placed me in my present predicament. Four seasons worth of suitors, and I had not found one who could hold his own with my formidable father and my very challenging brothers. I had no doubt Rochmont could. I blinked. But that chilling insight would not disappear. Rochmont could give me a year, two years, three years, and it was highly unlikely I would find a man who was both blindly devoted to me and whom I could respect in the presence of the men in my family!

"Constance, Constance, do not look so bleak! I have never heard the slightest whisper that Lord Rochmont is anything but honorable! Certainly Lord Chase would not have accepted his suit otherwise! And look at yourself!"

"I do, Drusilla, every day in the looking glass!"

"But I wager that you do not see what the rest of the world sees!"

"*Au contraire, ma cherie!* I see *precisely* what the rest of the world sees. Lady Constance Hatton: indulged, rich, passingly pretty in a blue-eyed blonde sort of way, no longer in the first blush of youth."

"Why Constance Hatton!" Drusilla exclaimed. "Never

would I have guessed that you, of all people would go fishing for compliments! And I hesitate to indulge you! But I
cannot think of a young lady of the *ton* who would not trade
places with you, even without your very impressive fiancé!
Look at the matter from Lord Rochmont's perspective. In
you, he has a wife who brings him a generous dowry—
something I daresay he neither cares about nor needs. More
importantly, he gains a wife who is an acknowledged beauty,
has the wit and grace to forestall any number of suitors without incurring scandal or ill will, and, not least of all, is a
member of one of the most respected families in England.
How could he do better for himself? And is he not known for
doing the very best for himself?"

"But I have always wished . . ."

Before I could broach the heart of my concerns to
Drusilla, the door was flung open without so much as a
knock, and a flurry of white raced over to where we sat and
jumped onto my lap.

"Sorry, I am sure, my lady," a red-faced Daisy panted.
"That little dog has sure enough run me a merry chase!"

I apologized to Daisy for her trouble, and assured her
Medora would be given a sufficiently brisk walk to take care
of some of that excessive energy.

Drusilla and I walked to Green Park, where Medora could
have plenty of scope for chasing birds or treeing squirrels,
her two favorite pastimes after eating. Our maids, Daisy and
Margie had the wit to stay at a reasonable distance so we
could engage in private conversation. But thankfully, we did
not return to the subject interrupted by Medora's impetuous
entrance.

Drusilla had given me a good deal to consider. The case
she had presented for the wisdom of my match with
Rochmont made great sense. And she seemed to believe he
harbored affection for me. Last night he had amply demon-
strated he harbored an appreciation of my charms, but I
longed to know what his feelings for me were. I could sense
myself slipping toward an acceptance of the inevitability of

our marriage. There was a great pull toward forgetting my questions and hesitations, and just letting myself believe in the powerful current of mutual attraction that had been so apparent on the terrace.

Drusilla, ever the perceptive friend, seemed to understand my preoccupation and kept up a steady flow of chatter to which I could respond without losing concentration on my private thoughts about a possible future as wife of Lord Rochmont.

When we reached the park, I let Medora off the leash, and she ran to and fro in front of us: first investigating what looked to be a mole's run, then putting to flight a flock of sparrows that had been innocently enjoying the sunshine. Next, a squirrel diverted her attention, which finally, growing tired of her pursuit, ran up a tree in the middle of a small grove some distance from the footpath. Medora collapsed at the bottom of the tree either from exhaustion or with the intent to wait the descent of the squirrel.

Clearly, it would take less effort to go and retrieve her than for us to tire ourselves urging her to leave her post. So Drusilla and I strolled across the grass to the small grove of trees where Medora lay panting. As I bent to fasten the leash, I heard Drusilla's sharp intake of breath. She stood as if frozen, looking across the lawn stretching down the slope on the other side of the grove where we were. I stood and looked where she was staring.

On a bench close to the Mall entrance of the park sat a couple. The man's back was to us as he turned to his companion, who was partially obscured, but her identity was clear. She was Lady Antony. And in spite of the fact that I could not see his face, I also knew for certain the man's identity. He was my fiancé, Lord Rochmont.

As Drusilla and I stood mesmerized, Lady Antony threw her arms about Rochmont's neck. I felt as if I had been struck. I turned, not wanting to witness another second of the scene, and ran toward the path leading back to Hatton House, dragging poor Medora with me.

By the time I reached the path, Drusilla had caught up with me.

"I am certain there is a perfectly reasonable explanation," my friend declared.

I tried to swallow, but my mouth was dry. I tried to catch my breath, but my heart was pounding.

"Certainly, there is an obvious explanation." I could hear my voice shake and took a deep breath. "Everyone knows that Rochmont has a preference for dashing widows. And there is no more dashing a widow than Lady Antony!"

"I think you are being unfair, jumping to that sort of conclusion," Drusilla protested stoutly.

"What other conclusion could there be?" I asked hotly, not even trying to spare my pride.

Drusilla stopped walking, forcing me to stop also. She regarded me patiently.

"Remember exactly what we saw. We saw Lady Antony throw her arms about Lord Rochmont's neck. We did not see him initiate an embrace."

For a second, the terrible weight that had settled over my heart lifted. How foolish I had been to leap to unhappy conclusions! But then, doubts and uncertainty returned, and so did the weight on my heart. Why had Rochmont been sitting on a bench in Green Park with Lady Antony? What, exactly was the nature of his friendship with her? It was obviously close, by the evidence of my own eyes. Even the most dedicated rakes forsook their mistresses during an engagement and the first few months of marriage. Not to was to inflict insult on their intended or new bride. Was he bidding Lady Antony a fond farewell? Or were her charms more than he could resist?

Drusilla resumed walking.

"Perhaps the best way to satisfy your curiosity, Constance, is to just mention to Lord Rochmont casually that you thought you might have seen him in Green Park this morning. He will, no doubt, be very open about matters, and you will discover that your fears are for nothing."

"I shall consider it."

How could I possibly risk my pride asking Rochmont such a question? What if he laughed and said that he had not been near Green Park?

Chapter Ten

Drusilla apologized for leaving me when I was feeling so low, but she had promised to accompany her Great Aunt Louisa shopping, an expedition that promised to be draining even for someone of my friend's high energy and spirits. I managed a genuinely sympathetic word for her in parting, but I was not sorry to be left alone. A day that had begun with such promise had turned challenging, and I knew I would best recoup my forces and plan for the afternoon's campaign in solitude.

I found the small sitting room overlooking the square in front of Hatton House deserted. Retrieving a piece of embroidery from a basket next to the settee, I realized I had not touched it since the afternoon I had waited in this very room to be summoned for my betrothal interview with Rochmont. A maid had evidently retrieved my thimble and had thoughtfully replaced my needle in the little sewing case that also contained my gold embroidery scissors. Her thoughtfulness, unfortunately, had not extended to unraveling the ugly knot, which punctuated a line of astoundingly irregular stitches.

Using the needle, I applied myself to untangling the knot. Surely it would have been simpler to merely cut it, rip the offending stitches, and begin anew. But, somehow, untangling the knot became a test of patience and endurance I could not abandon. As I worked, I assessed my situation.

Drusilla had recommended that I let Rochmont know I had been in Green Park that morning, and from his response, discover the nature of his encounter with Lady Antony. But I was not inclined to follow her advice. When had I ever been able to read his thoughts? Worse still, I was feeling much too brittle to disguise my own reaction if I caught Rochmont in an outright lie.

I carefully drew a strand out of the knot and began to loosen another.

How had I managed to arrive at such an unenviable place? When had my affections become engaged? How would I see matters through with my pride intact, if not my heart?

I separated a second strand with a gentle tug.

I determined to reveal nothing of my torment to Rochmont. He said he admired me for my deceptive wit. I determined to give him what he admired. If he could not love me, he would continue to appreciate my composure and aplomb. Of course, any further familiarities would have to be avoided. Keeping one's composure and aplomb was not possible when one was being kissed until one's knees buckled.

I stuck the needle into the heart of the knot and felt it loosening.

I remembered the matter of Daisy and Armand, this time with satisfaction. The first time I had mentioned his servant's attempted seduction of my maid had been a request for assistance. This time, I would have the advantage of being able to express disappointment in Rochmont's lack of success. Subtle recrimination would give me the upper hand. Perhaps I could imply he did not really care, or had neglected the matter completely. That might restore the balance in my favor in this disconcerting emotional duel with my fine French fiancé!

I delicately tugged at a strategic strand, and, *voila!* The knot unraveled. I quickly picked out the offending stitches, replaced the needle in its little case, and promised myself I would devote serious attention to creating a flawless work of embroidery art in the coming days.

My fine French fiancé arrived promptly at half past three. I suppose when one is coordinating encounters with more than one lady, punctuality helps to keep appointments straight. He showed every indication of appreciating the green sprigged peach muslin, and if he was not even more appreciative of seeing me, I could not detect it. I avoided any awkward moments of greeting by extending my hand and beaming at him well before he had an opportunity to draw me into an embrace. He betrayed no hint of noticing any coolness in my demeanor.

On the way to the park, I chatted away merrily about the *on dits* he had missed during his absence, knowing all the while that he probably could have cared less about Miss Standish's pug's encounter with Lord Obmismon's wolf-hound, or Louisa Fortesque giving the cut direct to Lord Floode, or the number of offers Cecily Stratton was said to have refused.

As we entered the park, I knew the time had come to broach the problem of Daisy and Armand.

"Rochmont, I am afraid I must once again address the matter of my maid and your manservant," I began in a solemn tone.

He pulled the carriage to the side of the lane, and the memory of our last conversation in that precise location made me realize my plan had not taken in all potential factors. This was where Rochmont had almost kissed me. It was too much to hope that Lady Norham would rescue me a second time.

I took a deep breath and tried to look hurt and regretful. I could not quite meet his eyes, so I gazed soulfully at a distant tree behind him.

"I loathe to bring this matter up a second time, Rochmont, but I am deeply concerned about my maid, Daisy."

I looked at him directly. His face betrayed nothing but patient concern. According to my plan, he was supposed to be slightly chagrined.

"As I mentioned to you before you left, Daisy has conceived an infatuation with your manservant, Armand. I had trusted that the separation would cool her interest."

"What possible evidence do you have that separation cools ardor, Constance?" His voice was a caress.

I desperately studied the tree while steadying my breath. Nothing was going according to plan. I abandoned all hope of placing this impossible man at a disadvantage and endeavored as best I could to rescue my gullible maid from the clutches of a continental rogue.

"You promised me you would speak to Armand, Rochmont! No doubt to you, the matter of a simple English country girl's heart is of little importance, but Daisy believes she is truly in love with your Armand. And I will not stand idly by and see the poor girl's heart broken!"

I could hear my voice getting higher as I spoke, and I had to blink unbidden tears away to keep Rochmont's face in focus.

I looked down and saw I had wrung my handkerchief into a rope. My companion silently offered me his.

"Constance, dear one, of course I care. I consider an English country girl's heart to be something worthy of the most assiduous attention."

I should have known better than to have glanced at his face then, but I did. The look in his coffee-colored eyes warmed me to my toes. I wanted to throw myself into his arms and bury my face in his snowy cravat. But fortunately, at that moment, he took my hand and I was able to steady myself with the strength his handclasp imparted.

He smiled softly and drew a finger down my cheek.

"You are not to worry about Daisy and Armand, Constance. I did speak most seriously with Armand. And he assures me that his intentions toward Daisy are entirely honorable. Indeed, as soon as the date of our wedding is announced, he plans to formally ask your permission to marry her. You do not object to Daisy's continuing as your maid after we are wed, do you? I certainly would not want to do without Armand's services. I believe there is much to be said for the convenience of our personal servants being married to each other."

I tried to hide my astonishment at the audacity of Rochmont's presuming that our marriage would, indeed, take place. He had given me twelve months to search for another, more suitable mate. But there was nothing tentative in his assumption that we would one day marry. I struggled unsuccessfully to find the proper words and tone to remind him of our private agreement. But the bland look of satisfaction on his face as he told me of the "solution" to the problem of Daisy and Armand's relationship made it difficult for me to bring up the matter.

"But you promised . . . !" I blurted out, again fighting tears.

He patted my hand as if consoling an unreasonable child.

"Of course, I remember our little agreement, and I can count days and weeks. But I took courage from our reunion last night. Foolish of me, perhaps, but there you have it."

He slowly raised my hand to his lips and lightly brushed my gloved knuckles with the softest of kisses, all the while mesmerizing me with his warm brown eyes.

"It is impossible for me to believe, *cherie,* that I would receive quite so—welcome a welcome if your heart was engaged to another."

He smiled his most engaging smile and prepared to set the horses in motion, but a magnificent chestnut galloping toward us captivated our immediate attention. As it neared, its rider slowed to a trot and halted neatly next to Rochmont.

What he lacked in grace and elegance in ballrooms and parlors, Ferdy Courlan more than made up when driving a team or sitting a horse. Although his hat was sitting at a precarious angle on the back of his head, his neck-cloth would have been an embarrassment to any self respecting valet, and his jacket, while tailored flawlessly, was an unbecoming dun color that hinted strongly of having been made up from a bolt of cloth rejected by more exacting gentlemen, Ferdy Courlan commanded respect, both for his taste in horseflesh and his skill with the high bred animals whose conformation qualified them for places in his much envied stables.

Sadly, as soon as he spoke, Ferdy's dignity evaporated.

"Morning, Lady Constance, Rochmont . . . er . . . that is, afternoon now, isn't it?"

He gazed up at the sun, apparently to determine how far it had progressed in its daily journey, and jammed his hat far forward on his brow when it threatened to fall off.

"That is an outstanding mount, even by your exacting standards, Courlan."

Rochmont's respectful tone restored Ferdy's confidence, and opened the one subject he could discuss with no hesitation or embarrassment.

He stroked the chestnut's neck with pride.

"Name's Zeus. Got him from Floode. Lucky timing, just before the poor s . . ." he glanced quickly at me and continued. "Poor soul had to leave for the continent."

Lord Floode was notorious for his debauchery and dishonesty, but to Ferdy Courlan, the penalty of having to part with such a specimen of equine perfection qualified the despised peer for sincere sympathy. Ferdy jammed his hat further down on his forehead and tugged at his neck-cloth.

"Actually, Lady Constance, I am very glad to see you here. Thought I might have to go to one of those at home thingies to catch a word with you. Not that Lady Chase's entertaining isn't . . . wonderfully . . . uh . . . entertaining, don'tcha know! But *at homes*—why they call them that, I never could quite figure out. Most of the folks at one are not at home at all—at other folks' homes, don'tcha know . . ."

Ferdy removed his hat and scratched his thinning hair as he puzzled over the problem of "at homes". He mopped his brow and settled his hat on the back of his head, where somehow, it suited him best. I smiled my encouragement. I had learned that any words I might speak at this juncture in an exchange with Ferdy Courlan risked extending the detour of Ferdy's thought processes, which wandered sufficiently without the introduction of new byways. But my fiancé evidently placed good manners before expediency.

"Perhaps you would like to speak alone with Lady Constance," Rochmont offered solicitously.

"No need for that!" was Ferdy's quick response, apparently close to panic at the thought of being left alone with me.

"Anyway," he continued, "the two of you are planning to be leg-shackled anyway . . . Uh . . . no offense, Rochmont . . . Oh, and you too, Lady Constance. If a fellow was about to be shackled, that is, uh . . . contemplating entering the Holy Estate of Matrimony . . . cannot think of a more agreeable lady than you, Lady Constance!" He concluded his ruminations on marital bliss with a ringing endorsement of my suitability as a wife.

"How dear of you to say so, Mr. Courlan," I beamed at him. "Should Lord Rochmont cry off, I shall keep your sentiments in mind!"

That was really too cruel of me. Evidently the thought of marrying me struck terror in poor Ferdy's heart.

"Lady Constance!" Ferdy's face had blanched a sickly shade of greyish white. He turned to Rochmont, eager to make amends. "No intent to poach on your turf, Rochmont, no intent at all. Lovely lady she is, but worship her from afar, don'tcha know!"

"No offense taken, Courlan," my companion reassured in calming tones. "Of course I agree with you that Lady Constance is most agreeable as a prospective wife," he turned to me with a wicked glint in his dark eyes, "with the tiny flaw of being a heartless flirt, which can, I admit, disturb a gentleman's tranquility."

"Well," Ferdy responded magnanimously, "if there is a fellow who can school a lady in proper respect for . . . well, in proper respect, don'tcha know, I believe you are the gentleman for the job!"

Having mended his fences with Rochmont, he turned to "reassure" me, oblivious to my reaction to being "schooled" by anyone, much less the infuriating man to whom I was promised in marriage.

"Lady Constance! I suppose you forgot: Gentlemen Don't Break Engagements!" He cited this as a rule memorized from some deportment text he had been forced to study as a lad.

"How right you are!" Rochmont agreed heartily with the self-satisfied Ferdy, who had the look of a village curate who had just made two squabbling children shake hands and cry friends.

"Connie, dearest sweetheart," my perfidious fiancé turned to me, lifting each of my hands for a delicate kiss, "never fear that I would ever, for a moment, wish for any end to our betrothal other than matrimony."

Rochmont wisely did not look at me directly. But I could see a wicked gleam in his dark eyes and he was barely suppressing a grin. It was a struggle not to dissolve into helpless laughter.

Ferdy gathered the chestnut's reigns and bestowed a beatific smile upon us in preparation to depart, when I remembered what had started our ridiculous conversation.

"Did you not have a matter you needed to discuss with me?" I asked Ferdy.

Ferdy's smile collapsed into an expression of undiluted misery.

"I need to make amends for . . . steering Lady Antony into that orange tree last night. And . . . I don't know how I can ever make it up to her. Couldn't find her at the ball . . . er . . . but then . . ." He blushed crimson and gulped. "Ripped her gown right down the back . . . should offer to pay . . . but chaps don't pay for ladies' gowns . . ." Another rule from the deportment book, no doubt.

He scratched the few wisps of hair remaining on his markedly high forehead.

"Still can't figure how that tree got to where it was . . ."

I intervened quickly to block Ferdy from digressing into a discussion of the growth habits of potted orange trees.

"Honestly, Mr. Courlan, I think you are worried for nothing. After all, you did apologize to Lady Antony at the time. It was an accident! I know she will not hold it against you!"

Ferdy's frown turned wistful. "You really believe so, Lady Constance? Pr'haps you're right. Lady Antony is as kind as she is beautiful. To think she would accept me as a partner for a dance!"

His expression turned to one of awe.

Little as I felt like lauding Lady Antony, I was moved to reassure poor Ferdy, who was genuinely distressed.

"If I were in your place, Mr. Courlan, I would just send round a note of apology and an offering of flowers. I am sure Lady Antony understands it was all just one of those unfortunate things that sometimes happens."

Finally, there was relief on Ferdy's face. "You think that'll put me in Lady Antony's good graces, Lady Constance?"

"I am certain of it, Mr. Courlan! As you said, Lady Antony is as kind as she is beautiful!"

"That she is." Ferdy looked pensive for a moment. "Not in the way of thinking of settling down, but if I was, Lady Antony would be the ideal . . . er . . . not that I would for a minute . . . presume . . . well . . . a lady like Lady Antony . . . she could have anyone she chose . . . not up to her standards . . ." Ferdy became flushed with embarrassment as he tried to express an affection that did not involve horses.

"Oh, there will be any number of disappointed gentlemen should Lady Antony ever again become particular in her affections, Courlan. You will have plenty of company," Rochmont reassured.

Ferdy Courlan finally took leave of us, apparently in better spirits than I as the result of our discussion of Lady

Antony's virtues. Since the subject of Lady Antony had already been introduced, I tried to decide how I might turn the conversation along the lines Drusilla had suggested. But Rochmont's voice intruded on my thoughts.

"Obviously, there is much that I admire in you, Constance."

I turned my face up to Rochmont's in response to these sentiments, much as a flower turns its face toward the warmth of the sun.

"And I especially admire your generosity of spirit."

I basked in his praise.

"Particularly in the case of Lady Antony."

Fortunately, the horses required his attention at that moment, so he didn't see the shock I know was reflected on my face.

"Whatever do you mean, Rochmont?" I managed.

We had left the park and Rochmont was speaking while attending to driving—thank heavens for small favors!

"As you must be painfully aware yourself, Constance, ladies of exceptional beauty are not always accorded kindness and understanding by ladies not so blessed. Jealousy is an insidious spoiler."

He turned to me and smiled. "I cannot tell you how pleased I am that you can see Lady Antony's true nature. Few ladies see beyond the superficial, to her basic goodness and courage."

"Why, Rochmont! How very dear of you to pay me such a compliment."

I prayed he would interpret my stunned expression as my being overwhelmed by his tribute. But I was not too stunned to recognize the gift of a perfect opening when it was handed to me. I knew, though, I would have to tread carefully. Even admiration for my superior discernment and generosity of spirit would not rob Rochmont of his keen powers of observation.

"I think it is charming of you to champion Lady Antony's cause. Although, I must say, I did not know that you had more than a passing acquaintance with her."

For a moment, Rochmont looked surprised, then shrugged and smiled his half smile.

"I seem to forget how little we actually know of each other. Madeleine—that is Lady Antony—and I have been acquainted since the year of her come-out. Let me see now. That would have been a year before your triumphant debut on the social scene."

He let his attention wander from the horses long enough to favor me with an appreciative glance.

"Lord Antony and I had shared interests, horses, hunting, that sort of thing you know," he continued.

And ladies of a certain disposition, too, no doubt.

"He was quite the ladies' man."

I had to admire how neatly Rochmont had assigned that characteristic to his friend without admitting it himself.

"So, you can imagine how amazed everyone was when he proposed marriage to Miss Madeleine Sedgewick mere days after he had been presented to her. A feat, I might add, accomplished with supreme guile and planning, for no watchful Mama would have willingly exposed her precious darling to Lord Antony's wiles."

Just as no watchful Mama would have willingly exposed her precious darling to my companion's wiles, I thought silently.

"Was it a happy marriage?"

No harm in adding to my knowledge of a lady my fiancé openly admired.

He gave me the bland glance I found so frustrating.

"Ultimately, who knows the presence or absence of happiness in a marriage but the partners? And even they might differ in their assessment." Rochmont punctuated this observation with a Gallic shrug.

"They clearly felt intensely about each other. And Lord Antony surprised us all by being an absolutely faithful husband, as fidelity is commonly understood."

Did Blaise de Grenault, Lord Rochmont share in this common understanding of fidelity, I wondered?

"But he had not earned the sobriquet wild for nothing. He had always been a gambler, gambling for high stakes in London hells. He gave that up, along with the pursuit of petticoats. But he took to wagering on death-defying challenges. Swimming to a certain rock two miles off a rugged coast at the turning of a high tide, that sort of thing. Madeleine could count on his coming home at night, but sometimes he was not conscious. And it had nothing to do with drink."

"I had heard that his death was due to a fall . . . from a horse, I think?" I decided to help Rochmont's narrative along.

He nodded.

"Ironic, is it not? I have never known a more skilled horseman. But he accepted a wager that he could ride the perimeter of his principal estate from midnight to sun-up. It was a full moon, but a storm blew in obliterating any light. His horse stumbled into a trench newly dug to drain a wet field. Madeleine was inconsolable. And young Tony was but a babe. To make matters worse, the Compton family was determined to dictate the terms of Tony's rearing—he stands second in line to the title, you know. And no one ever accused the Comptons of reasonableness."

He pulled up the team neatly in front of Hatton House. A stable lad came running and Rochmont threw him the reins as he continued his story.

"I am certain that the Duke and Duchess thought that they could dictate to Madeleine, but in her quiet way, she ran rings around them. Charmed them. Smiled and nodded as they nattered on. Made subtle suggestions that they came to believe were their own ideas."

Rochmont favored me with his rare, beaming smile.

"Merciful heavens, how I do adore watching a devious female mind in action!"

He punctuated his declaration by kissing me resoundingly on the mouth, much to the stable lad's interest.

Rochmont handed me down and as we mounted the stairs

to Hatton House, I was about to offer him some refreshment in order to sound him out more completely about his relationship with the fair Madeleine. But Perkins scotched my plan.

"My lord," he bowed to Rochmont. "Lord Chase would like a word with you, if you have a moment."

Chapter Eleven

As I entered my bedroom, I noticed that Daisy had a fresh nosegay of daisies and forget-me-nots pinned to her fichu. Undoubtedly, with the slightest encouragement, she would have given me a fulsome account of her receipt of the flowers. But something in my demeanor must have silenced even the loquacious Daisy, because she quietly closed the curtains and turned down my bed when I informed her of my need to rest.

If only my brain had responded to my request with equal efficiency. I felt like a fair juggler who had put one too many balls in the air. Why was it so difficult to order my own romantic life? I had quietly managed the romantic lives of any number of acquaintances over the past years and everything had worked out very much to my satisfaction. Now, when my own happiness was at issue, my skills seemed to have deserted me.

I must have spoken my concerns aloud, for Medora, who was resting on a brocade slipper chair raised her head and blinked inquiringly at me. But when she saw that no treat was forthcoming, she resumed her nap. The creature showed no loyalty, no gratitude. The least she could do was a little pacing to demonstrate some concern for my plight. I was clearly on my own.

Why had Papa requested a chat with Rochmont? What could they possibly have to discuss—other than me, or my dowry? Was Papa going to start pressing us to set a wedding date? Now I would have to apply myself to encouraging my frustrating fiancé to tell me what he had discussed with Papa. I knew it was useless to attempt to wheedle the information out of Papa. I could picture his response if I tried.

"Constance, m'dear, nothing to bother your pretty head about," Papa would say, without glancing up from his newspaper or his soup, or whatever was more worthy of his attention at the moment.

At least Rochmont had never said anything as patronizing to me. I could depend upon him to give me his undivided attention if I asked for it—sometimes even if I did not.

A feeling of well-being, a sense of being respected, even being valued washed over me. Amazingly, the man I called frustrating was the very first gentleman of my acquaintance who treated me as an adult, an adult with her own point of view and concerns. And when I had presented him with problems—the dream of marrying for love, the crush that my simple country maid had for his sophisticated manservant—he had listened attentively, and applied himself to satisfactory solutions. The fact that those solutions had not necessarily satisfied me, was not something for which he was to blame, I was forced to admit.

I was also forced to admit what made the gentleman frustrating was that he consistently treated me as an adult, as an equal! The thought was, at first, astonishing, and then truly, profoundly terrifying!

As a child, I had loved playing games: charades, jackstraws, hide-and-go-seek. And the games I played among the *ton* required no more effort than those nursery games. Because no one expected Lady Constance Hatton to have a serious thought under her golden curls or behind her sparkling smile. No one, until I met Rochmont that fateful April evening.

It is quite one thing to scheme and manipulate when no one suspects you are capable of such a thing, and quite another when someone catches you in the act and assumes you can continue acting perfectly normal while under his clear-eyed scrutiny. It was like playing draughts all one's life, and then being expected to play chess, with no instruction or practice.

Apparently, Rochmont expected me to cope with his enigmatic ways, his intrusive past, and his distracting kisses by simply adjusting to his level of gamesmanship. But I was floundering, my skills entirely inadequate to maintain an advantage with him that I had taken for granted with other gentlemen. The mocking faces of Lady Norham and Lord Cathcart rose unbidden and unwelcome. They knew both Rochmont and me also. Their pity was humiliating.

There was another option to continuing my game: to simply cease playing games, at least with Rochmont, the man who had not been fooled when practically everyone else was. But the idea of disarming myself with him threatened to send me into panic. I took several deep breaths and forced myself to look at the facts dispassionately.

Fact: I was engaged to marry Blaise de Grenault, Lord Rochmont, a man whom I scarcely knew, who showed every indication of admiring my person and my wit, but showed no indication of being at all in love with me.

Fact: Even during his absence, I had been unable to find a suitable replacement for Rochmont as a fiancé, and could not name one prospect that did not bore, disgust, or frighten me.

Fact: There were large and significant portions of Rochmont's life of which I was ignorant. These included his relationships with any number of ladies, and, apparently, a closer relationship with my own father than I had heretofore suspected.

Fact: Somehow, in a remarkably short time and even without being in the same town, Rochmont had managed to become the focus of my daytime thoughts and my nighttime dreams.

Fact: I did not want to break my engagement to Rochmont.

I sat straight up in bed. Was that, indeed a fact? How long

had I been shielding myself from this dreadful truth? My heart was pounding. I felt light-headed. I had to remind myself to breathe—the frustrating man seemed to have that effect on me.

I slowly lay back against the pillows and watched tiny dust motes dance in the narrow shafts of light filtering through the closed curtains. Honesty, even with oneself, can be exhausting. I needed distraction and sustenance. I rang for Daisy to help me dress in a plain blue muslin gown, and asked her to bring tea to the small parlor. Setting some perfect stitches was just what I needed to clear my mind, and a cup of tea and a hot muffin would restore my strength.

I chose a green silk thread and had completed a flawless leaf in chain stitch when tea and muffins arrived. Medora, who had roused herself sufficiently to accompany me to the parlor, cast a disparaging glance at the muffins I had ordered, and decided to try her luck elsewhere, padding out of the sitting room behind the servant who had delivered my tray.

I poured myself a cup of tea and strolled idly over to the window overlooking the front portal and the square. As I stood sipping tea, and watching carriages pass by, a gentleman descended the front steps of Hatton House. The gentleman's face was not visible, but just before he put on his top hat, his pale blond hair caught the afternoon light, making it seem that he wore a halo. Lord Cathcart. The teacup slipped. I was able to catch it without its falling and breaking, but I spilled tea all down the front of my gown. What business had Lord Cathcart with any inhabitant of Hatton House?

I took a napkin from the tea table and blotted at the huge tea stain on my gown.

"Whatever happened, Constance?"

Rochmont's voice startled me so, the napkin went flying in the air. He caught it neatly and offered it to me with a bow. I snatched it unceremoniously and tossed it on the table.

"You frightened me half out of what wits I possess, Rochmont. Had you considered knocking?"

I collapsed on the sofa.

Without invitation, he made himself comfortable beside me and took my cold hand in his.

"I had thought to surprise you."

"You did that for certain," I responded petulantly.

He raised my hand to his lips and I felt their warm, firm pressure. Then he enfolded my hand in both of his. I resisted an impulse to curl up closely beside him and rest my weary head on his sturdy shoulder.

"Will you not tell me what is troubling you, *cherie*?" he asked in silken tones.

An invitation to unburden my soul. An invitation to make myself as vulnerable to him as Daisy was to Armand.

He responded to my slight tug and released my hand.

"Obviously," I gestured toward my tea-stained gown.

"But you had not spilled tea on that fetching peach number you were wearing earlier."

"Nothing was troubling me earlier." I lied.

His raised eyebrow told me that he did not believe me.

A distraction was called for.

"But where are my manners?" I asked brightly. "I have offered you no refreshment."

He stayed my hand as I reached for the bell.

"No need."

I realized that there was about him a whiff of fine cigars and brandy. He and Papa had discussed whatever they had discussed with a degree of relaxation and cordiality if Papa had shared his best store of cigars and brandy.

"Of course not," I agreed brightly. "I can offer you neither the cigars nor the brandy that Papa can."

"But then, what you can offer, your papa cannot."

His bland expression belied the impropriety of his words. Clearly he was not referring to cold tea and muffins.

Rochmont had to notice my flushed face. Indeed, even my hands were quite warm. But I chose to ignore his gambit.

"I must admit," I was trying for the lightest, most unconcerned tone, "that I was a little bit curious about why my father should ask to see you."

"But of course you are curious, Constance, my dear. I should be astonished if you were ever without curiosity." He answered in as light a tone.

"You are teasing me, Rochmont."

"Sympathetic concern had no effect," he responded matter-of-factly.

"On second thought, perhaps I could use a little refreshment," he added, strolling to a tray of decanters across the room and choosing one.

"Constance, darling, is it so great a mystery what a prospective father-in-law might wish to discuss with his prospective son-in-law?"

He began to pour himself a drink.

"With Lord Cathcart present?"

Rochmont stopped pouring and looked up at me slowly, his face a bland mask. He said nothing, but resumed pouring, and then walked quietly back to the sofa and seated himself next to me once more. He sipped his drink and shrugged, then placed his glass on the small table next to him. He gazed out the window overlooking our front doorstep and glanced at the small tea stain on the carpet next to the window.

"What a convenient look-out spot," he observed appreciatively. "But why should seeing Cathcart departing Hatton House cause you to spill tea, Constance?" His eyes narrowed. "Did Cathcart make a nuisance of himself while I was abroad?"

"Nothing I was not capable of stifling." I dismissed my trials with Cathcart with a wave of the hand. I did not want to be deflected from my present inquiry. "Lord Cathcart was with you and Papa, was he not." It was a statement, not a question.

"Well, yes, he was, but last I knew, he is received by everyone." Rochmont studied me. "Just what is upsetting you, Constance? I cannot help if I do not know the problem."

The problem. How many problems were there? Lady Antony. Papa's conversation with Rochmont. Papa's conversation with Rochmont and Lord Cathcart. Rochmont and Cathcart's conversation about . . . Countess Magda? My imagination was getting out of hand and the silence needed to be broken. I would need to proceed cautiously. Telling an outright lie to Rochmont was not a course that recommended itself.

I set my face into a look of mild concern. "I heard talk that you and Lord Cathcart did not cry friends. It startled me to think that the two of you were meeting here with Papa."

Not anywhere near the whole truth, but not a lie either.

Rochmont visibly relaxed and cupped my face in his hands.

"Poor Connie," he said softly, and kissed me gently on the forehead before releasing me and settling back in the sofa.

"I am very sorry to have left you to the mercy of all the gossips so soon after our engagement."

How could a man with such a naturally harsh countenance arrange his features to look so kind?

"It is true," Rochmont continued, "Cathcart and I have not been the best of friends. An old matter that has ceased to matter. Some have suggested we are too much alike."

Now that was a thought I did not wish to contemplate for so much as a minute!

"Surely not!" I exclaimed without thinking.

Rochmont smiled expansively.

"So long as you prefer me," he raised his glass in a salute.

"What in the world could you and Papa and Lord Cathcart have been discussing?"

"That, my dear, I am not at liberty to say."

"But . . ."

"Constance, sweetheart," Rochmont once more enveloped my hand in his. I could feel the diamond on my engagement ring press into his palm.

"I must ask you to trust me. If matters work out so that we do marry, we would have to learn to trust each other in order to have any kind of livable life together. Why not practice now—just in case?"

"This exercise in trust appears to be rather one-sided," I protested feelingly.

"How can you say such a thing?"

It required hearing far more acute than mine to detect any hint of insincerity in Rochmont's question.

Because I saw Lady Antony throw herself into your arms just this morning, I wanted to scream.

"Just when have I ever asked you to trust me about anything?" I heard the acid in my tone and knew Rochmont did too.

"Admittedly, you did not ask me to trust you while I was away. But surely, unless the *ton* has changed its ways beyond recognition in a remarkably short period, the absence of a fiancé signals the declaration of open season on his fair lady by all bachelors of a certain reputation. Add to that my knowledge that you, my fair one, would be using the time of my absence to search out potential replacements for my role as future husband . . ."

Rochmont shrugged and tossed off the rest of his drink.

"The best I could hope for, if a replacement were found, was discretion on your part," he added.

Was that actually a hint of sadness in his eyes, or was it a trick of the late afternoon light?

"And just where were you during your absence from London society?" I could not afford to let myself sympathize with Rochmont.

He gave me a tired smile and chucked me under the chin.

"Ah, Connie, my sweet, you know I would have told you if I could."

"I know nothing of the sort!" I turned my face away from Rochmont and blinked rapidly to dispel the tears I could feel prickling the back of my eyes.

A large white handkerchief was placed in my hand. But I could not trust myself to raise it to dab my eyes for fear the tears I felt would break loose into uncontrollable sobs if I let down my guard so much as to acknowledge their presence. I knew Rochmont was studying me as I sat there, stiff backed, refusing to look in his direction.

If I crumbled now, I might as well resign myself to a life-time living at the mercy of Rochmont's wiles. That was precisely where I knew it would end if he got even a hint that I cared about him or his doings. A quick change of tone was called for.

"Heavens! I do beg your pardon, Rochmont! I cannot think what possessed me to make such a piece of work over personal business of yours that does not concern me in the least! Mama always warned that those novels I read from Hookham's would undermine any common sense I might have. Can I freshen your drink?"

All I could hope was that my limbs would not shake too badly to carry me across the room.

My companion did not try to disguise his satisfaction.

"Thank you, no, Connie. I believe I have had quite enough brandy for one afternoon, particularly if I wish to keep my wits about me, which I find is essential when I am with you."

I knew he was flattering me, but I could not resist the warm glow I felt at his words. The smile I gave him was genuine.

"Oh, Connie, Connie, Connie." Rochmont pulled me into his arms and I did not—could not—resist. He kissed my brow, my eyelids, which were closed in languid heaviness. And then, at last, he kissed my mouth. How I had missed his kisses. How long had it been? Weeks? Days? No, just hours. He traced a line of kisses from my mouth to my ear.

"I think it is quite satisfactory for you to care about my personal concerns. Very satisfactory indeed," he whispered.

"Constance!" Mama stood in the doorway, a large white envelope in her hand.

Rochmont was on his feet, bowing.

"Lady Chase."

"Lord Rochmont." Mama extended her hand.

"Forgive me for intruding," Mama appeared anything but shocked or distressed. "I thought you might be interested in this invitation, Constance, my love. But I am sure that no interruption is welcome when young people are making wedding plans."

She smiled at us benignly, placed the envelope on the tea tray, and exited, closing the door behind her.

What can I say? I could have beaten my brains out or laughed. I laughed. Uncontrollably. Rochmont laughed. I had never seen him laugh like that before, hand on hips, head thrown back. I tried valiantly to regain my composure, but my efforts were in vain. At last all I could do was bury my face in the handkerchief Rochmont had thoughtfully provided earlier and give way to gale after gale of full-throated laughter. I struggled for control, but each time I thought the storm of merriment was subsiding, I would catch Rochmont's eye, and we would both go off into whoops again.

The hairpins that had begun to be loosened by his attentions earlier were now falling about me on the sofa. I collected them as I endeavored to collect my composure and walked over to the only looking glass in the room, a convex thing called a bull's eye that afforded only a small reflection, and a distorted one at that. I gathered my hair into a loose knot and struggled to anchor it as best I could on the top of my head.

"No," Rochmont, who had moved directly behind me, said softly.

I turned, mouth full of hairpins, arms upraised holding my topknot in place.

"I'mmmst gt mhrr'p" I tried to explain around the pins.

He smiled and removed the pins from my mouth one at a time, tossing them on the floor and placed my arms around his neck.

"Oh, no, my dear Connie, you must not put your hair up, because I have longed to see you with it down."

He lazily twisted a strand around his index finger.

"Silken sunshine," he murmured and brought it to his lips.

I expected to be pulled into a fast embrace and to be kissed senseless—at least that is what I very much wanted to happen. But instead, he held me loosely, idly stroking the hair that had tumbled about my shoulders.

"For all her blatant manipulation, Constance, your mama has the right of it." He looked at me steadily. "We really should set a wedding date."

I was about to suggest that the banns be read the very next Sunday, or perhaps the purchase of a special license, when, mercifully, the picture of Rochmont with Lady Antony flashed in my mind's eye. I stiffened and backed away.

"Before any wedding plans are made, perhaps you should know that I was in Green Park this morning!" I blurted out.

For a moment, all that showed on Rochmont's face was baffled confusion, then understanding seemed to dawn on him.

"The mystery of your coolness this afternoon is solved then." He said levelly. "But I did mention, did I not, that Lady Antony is an old friend of mine."

"That was apparent!"

"Connie, my sweet, this is all just a misunderstanding."

Rochmont took my hand, but I refused to respond to his touch.

"Can you tell me, then, just what it was that you and Lady Antony were discussing this morning in Green Park?" I asked him challengingly.

"I am afraid I cannot, Constance. I gave my word." He sounded genuinely regretful.

"Then, I am afraid I cannot discuss a wedding date, Rochmont."

"If I were able to tell you, would you set a date, Constance?"

No wonder this man was so successful in commerce. He never ceased to bargain.

"That would depend entirely on the nature of your discussion with Lady Antony, would it not?" I replied with as much hauteur as I could summon.

Rochmont smiled and patted my cheek.

"You know something, sweetheart? I think we are making progress. I am very much encouraged."

"How felicitous for you!" I threw at him in frustration. "I am afraid I must excuse myself. I must rest before facing Mrs. Edgar Beaufort's musicale this evening. I have had a most trying day!"

I meant to sweep from the room and slam the door behind me. But Rochmont was there first, opening the door and bowing me out. Certainly he could have spared me that self-satisfied smile as he bid me adieu.

Chapter Twelve

If I had acted upon my inclination, I would have sent regrets to Mrs. Beaufort instead of attending her musicale. I do enjoy music, and Mrs. Beaufort has both the taste and means to hire the very best musicians for her annual entertainment. Indeed, if the evening were to be devoted only to music, I would have looked forward to being soothed and refreshed. But, of course, most in attendance would be there to be seen and to gossip rather than to be uplifted by the artistry of the performers. And since it was less than twenty-four hours since Rochmont's return, I could count on being a focus of gossip if I absented myself.

As I lay upon my bed with a cloth dampened with lavender water pressed to my brow, it was hard for me to realize it had been less than a full day since my betrothed had come striding across the Duchess of Fanshawe's ballroom floor, changing my life from being just manageable into being totally beyond my control. And Mama was pressing for a wedding date. Once I had granted her that, I would be pulled into a whirlwind that would sweep me up and deposit me at the altar of St. George's at the appointed hour. I wanted answers to some questions before I would give myself willing to such a fate.

Daisy had the wit to spare me her usual prattle as she helped me dress for the evening. I rewarded her by accepting her first suggestion for my gown—a sheer royal blue silk,

148

falling in tiers trimmed in broad bands of lace. For jewelry, I wore every pearl I owned.

I was stunned when Jack presented himself to escort Mama and me for the evening. Musicales had never been his idea of an evening's entertainment. And, even more surprisingly, instead of humoring him, as Mama was want to do when he played the part of dutiful son and brother, she used the carriage ride to the Beaufort's townhouse to admonish Jack for his appearance and choice of companionship the night before.

"I vow, Jack, I have never been so humiliated by the behavior of one of my children!" Mama stated dramatically, hand on her ample bosom.

"Come now, Mama, surely at least one of the occasions when I was sent home from school distressed you as much," Jack replied languidly.

"Do not think you can distract me with memories of your childhood pranks," Mama replied with a dismissive wave of the hand. "To begin with, that costume you wore last night bordered on indecent! I would not have permitted you to escort Constance and me to the ball, had I not been rendered speechless when I first saw it!"

"Darling, Mama," Jack cajoled. "It would take considerably more than a Corsair's ensemble to deprive you of speech. And, furthermore, I can think of at least ten classically inspired costumes that rendered mine positively puritanical. You know quite well that those ridiculously ballooned trousers were far less revealing of my limbs than what I am wearing right now."

"You are being indelicate, Jack," Mama reproved.

"My apologies, Mama, Connie. I suppose I relaxed my guard, what with Connie being engaged."

Jack was going to make an outstanding diplomat. He already had the knack of apologizing while questioning one's basic common sense and shifting the focus of conversation to someone else.

But Mama has never been that easily vanquished.

"As you say, Jack, your sister is engaged, and as such is prepared to assume a responsible role in society."

How deflating to hear my betrothal reduced to such mundane purposes. But at least Jack remained the primary target of Mama's remarks.

"Look at you, Jack, many years her senior, showing no indication of settling your interests on a *marriageable* lady."

Even in the dim light of the carriage, I did not dare meet Jack's eye for fear of losing my composure. Either of us could have recited that sentence by heart. We had heard it, in various permutations since Justin, our eldest brother, had shown some reluctance to court the misses of Mama's selection.

"One of these days, Jack," Mama continued, "you will wake to discover that you have been entrapped by a manifestly unsuitable female, and there will be *nothing*," predictably, Mama's tones became tinged with tragedy at this juncture, "*nothing* either your father or I can do to rescue you!"

"I appreciate your concern, Mama, truly I do. But there really is nothing for which you need be concerned," Jack reassured.

"Nothing for which to be concerned! Jack! That creature! That flame-haired creature! Everyone,"—by 'everyone', Mama meant all of her fellow matrons and chaperones—"everyone was whispering, and I could positively feel their pity!"

"Please, Mama! Spare my *amour propre*!" Jack steadfastly refused to be drawn into our parent's ploy. "Certainly you grant me sufficient wit to avoid a serious entanglement with the devious Thérèse! Furthermore, as you well know, even if I lacked the wit, I would be safe. As I believe I pointed out to you before, Lady Norham is in need of replenishing her coffers, and a younger son's portion would not do for that."

Mama sniffed. "Even if that is the case, and, mind you, I am not for a moment accepting it is, you are wasting valuable time, Jack, time that should be spent with young ladies of faultless breeding and decorum! And, it pains me to add, time spent in such activities would also serve to add some luster to peoples' perception of your character, which, deserved or not, has been ever so slightly tarnished by the carefree attitude that you affect. Not everyone can see beyond the superficial, Jack, to your seriousness of purpose."

Seriousness of purpose! Did Mama truly believe that Jack possessed any seriousness of purpose beyond his pursuit of amusement? Or was she rehearsing something to say to her fellow matrons and chaperones? Our arrival at the Beaufort's relieved me from having to solve that puzzle.

I confess that even on an occasion when one had contemplated staying home, entering a perfectly appointed house staffed by discreet servants and surrounded by one's elegantly gowned and tailored friends, caused one's spirits to be lifted. The *ton* might exact a price for belonging, a price paid in being the focus of unwanted attention and the need to summon reserves of energy just to maintain one's social standing, but with whom would I wish to change places? Certainly not Daisy or her sister Prim.

"Lady Constance! I vow I was *longing* to see you so I could tell you just how *thrilled* I am for you that Lord Rochmont has returned from his journeying, and I know you must be thrilled too!"

The shrill voice of Althea Sandforth was instantly recognizable—and audible to most in attendance.

"But, my gracious, did he not accompany you tonight?"

Speaking of the price paid to belong to the *ton*, Althea Sandforth was well on her way to becoming one its most prominent dues collectors. She really did need to work on her tone of false sympathy. But subtlety would elude her forever, I suspected.

I managed a bright smile.

"Miss Sandforth, my dear! How charming of you to share in my joy at Lord Rochmont's safe return! And, no, he did

not accompany me tonight. We find we are both happier if
we do not live in one another's pockets, which, I am sure you
will discover is the case when you become engaged."

A brief narrowing of Miss Sandforth's eyes gave me the
satisfaction of knowing she had noted my gentle rebuke.
But, Lady Sandforth, usually on the alert for the tiniest slight
of her daughter, failed to react, her attention being drawn to
the newest arrivals. Soon the hallway leading to Mrs. Beaufort's music room was a buzz as people took note as "That
Flame-Haired Creature"—Lady Norham—dressed in peach
silk, which featured expansive décolletage, entered on the
arm of Lord Bamwell, who appeared to be holding an
earnest conversation with said décolletage. I felt Mama
stiffen and glance at Jack, who, rather than displaying any
jealousy, looked amused.

"You see that your fears were for naught, Mama," he re-
marked softly.

"I see nothing of the sort," Mama fairly sputtered.

In Mama's personal view of social relations, the entire
population of the opposite sex must adore her children, and
the defection of any admirer, eligible or not, is recorded as a
personal affront.

"Captain Hatton, I vow, how delightful to see you this
evening!"

Althea Sandforth's eyelash batting was no more subtle
than her feigned sympathy.

"Miss Sandforth," Jack turned on the full force of his
charm for her benefit. "How you maintain your radiance after the rigors of last night's ball is a marvel."

I imagined at that moment, Mama was balancing the ad-
vantages of having a daughter-in-law with a dowry of leg-
endary magnitude against the disadvantages of having a
daughter-in-law with taste and elegance just slightly above
that of a fishmonger. But such calculations were a waste of
time, for when Jack had "assisted" us all to seats, Miss Sandforth found herself sandwiched between her mama and me,
with Jack sitting on the aisle, on the other side of Mama. Ob-

viously, he did not wish to be the recipient of Althea's asides during the concert. Miss Sandforth's reaction to this seating arrangement reminded me of Medora's when one eats the last bite of cake she had coveted.

Although I was a poor substitute for Jack, Miss Sandforth was unable to restrain herself from enlightening me with her reactions to and opinions of all of the goings-on in the *ton*. She nodded to where Lady Antony, serene in lavender silk and amethysts, sat between Ferdy Courlan and Major Howells.

"Lady Constance, have you *ever* witnessed anything as shocking as Mr. Courlan's practically ripping Lady Antony's gown off her body last night! I promise you, I was so overcome, I might have fainted dead away!"

I took this to mean she regretted her decision to scream rather than faint, which would have had the advantage of forcing Jack to carry her from the dance floor. But I could not let the implied charge against poor Ferdy stand unchallenged.

"You must not have had as clear a view of the incident as I, Miss Sandforth. I promise you it was entirely an accident. Mr. Courlan, I believe, was even more distressed than Lady Antony. Regardless, Major Howells acted so quickly, she was spared the worst embarrassment. And just look, she obviously bears Mr. Courlan no ill will."

"Why she fails to is a mystery to me," Althea responded darkly. "A little more care for her reputation for delicacy would serve Lady Antony's long-term interests, I am sure. It quite escapes me why she is held as an example of irreproachable behavior."

I was about to suggest that Lady Antony was held as an example of irreproachable behavior because her behavior was, indeed, irreproachable, when Miss Sandforth gasped and clutched my arm, nodding at the couple taking their places on the aisle in the row in front of us. It was none other than Lady Norham and Lord Bamwell. Jack greeted them cordially. Mama favored Lord Bamwell with an icy smile, and granted Lady Norham a hint of a nod. I wondered idly

how Lady Norham could maintain her look of fascination at
Lord Bamwell's conversation, and how Lord Bamwell could
fail to detect the censure of the audience. Lady Norham,
never one to care much for others' opinion of her, ignored
glares and raised eyebrows.

"One would think," Miss Sandforth hissed. But, I was
spared hearing what one would think by Mrs. Beaufort,
who introduced The Riggatelli String Quartet, our evening's entertainment.

Their music making was so sublime, that, amazingly,
even Althea Sandforth was sufficiently under their spell to
forego her usual chatter. And, surprisingly, I, enthralled by
their celestial strains, enjoyed a true respite from my cares
and concerns. An all too brief respite, for, during intermission, I found myself by Jack's side, engaged in conversation
with Lord Bamwell and Lady Norham.

Lord Bamwell laboriously ascertained that both Jack and
I had previously made Lady Norham's acquaintance. We assured him that we had.

"But of course, Lady Constance, you are engaged to be
married to a fellow countryman of Lady Norham's, are you
not?" Lord Bamwell inquired needlessly.

"A quite brave lady, *non*?" Lady Norham gave me a con-
descending grimace.

"And of course, Captain Hatton and I were acquainted in
Paris."

She caressed Jack with her eyes, but Lord Bamwell, eager
to impress us with his acumen apparently did not notice her
open flirtation with another man.

"Ah, speaking of Paris, I hear King Louis is failing fast, not
physically, mind you, but not quite up to snuff in the old brain
box, don'tcha know," Lord Bamwell confided knowingly.

"My lord . . ." Lady Norham began.

"Is that a fact?" Jack asked mildly, ignoring Lady
Norham. "Don't recall hearing anything about him going
around the twist when I was last in Paris."

"Well, maybe not completely around the twist," Lord

Bamwell temporized. "Just not as sharp as one needs to be to deal effectively with the hoi-polloi who got into the habit of living above their station during the years of the Bourbons' exile."

"My lord!" Lady Norham tried again, bosom heaving, but Jack and Lord Bamwell were impervious.

"Don't say that they're spoiling for another fight over there. Prinny will be displeased after spending all that treasure in men and gold to put old Louis back on the throne. Wouldn't want to hear Wellington on the subject either." Jack sounded serious.

"No need for any bloodshed, that's the beauty . . ." Lord Bamwell began reassuringly, but Lady Norham was determined.

"My lord, there is Mr. Courlan, and you know you were most eager to discuss that gelding he acquired from Lord Poole's stable."

Lord Bamwell looked blank as if he had never heard of a gelding Ferdy Courlan had acquired from Lord Poole's stable. But Lady Norham wasted no time in summoning Mr. Courlan, so it was clear we would be changing the topic of conversation from French politics to horseflesh.

Shortly after greeting Ferdy, I drifted away, idly nodding to other guests, but preoccupied with what Lord Bamwell had been trying to say that Lady Norham seemed determined for him not to say. It sounded rather like the bits of conversation between Jack and Papa that I had overheard.

"You look perilously close to frowning, my dear. And, really, you must refrain. You owe it to all of your admirers to preserve your beauty for as long as possible."

The bored drawl was unmistakably Lord Cathcart's.

I was caught momentarily speechless, for I had not previously noticed Lord Cathcart in attendance, and his presence was every bit as surprising as Jack's had been.

"Tell me, Lady Constance," Lord Cathcart continued, ignoring my silence, "Is that incipient frown due to the absence of your betrothed? Or do you have other worries?

Either way," he bowed slightly, "I would be more than happy to do my best to lighten your spirits. A turn in the garden, perhaps?"

He smiled confidently and offered his hand.

"Thank you, but no, I really do not believe accompanying you into the garden would do anything but add to my concerns, my lord," I said with weary candor.

"Concerns. May I take it then your worries include more than your oft absent husband-to-be?"

Cathcart's drawl sounded as bored as usual, but I detected an unusual spark of interest in his cold, hooded eyes.

"Concern is probably too strong a word, my lord," I allowed. "But I admit some puzzlement over an extraordinary conversation involving, of all people, Lord Bamwell and Lady Norham."

I sensed Lord Cathcart's interest was now fully engaged.

"Bamwell and the devious Thérèse! Now there is a intriguing duet!"

"Surely, you could not have missed their dramatic entry, my lord!"

"Regrettably, I did, having just arrived. How unkind of fate to cheat me of one of the more memorable scenes of the season. Thérèse and Bamwell . . ."

Cathcart appeared to be lost for a moment or two, trying to conjure a picture of the unlikely couple. Then, once more, I felt the full force of his attention.

"And, what, pray tell, was the topic of the extraordinary conversation between that astonishing pair?"

Lord Cathcart's bored drawl did not adequately disguise an intensity quite unlike his usual disengagement.

"To be precise, the conversation was not just between Lord Bamwell and Lady Norham. Jack and I were included. Particularly Jack."

Was I imagining, or did Lord Cathcart relax ever so slightly? But having begun to discuss the matter, I found myself eager to share my bewilderment with someone who would listen.

"Lord Bamwell was intent on talking about King Louis of France. And, I promise you, Lady Norham was every bit as intent upon discussing anything else. She actually recruited Ferdy Courlan to discuss horses, in order to quiet Lord Bamwell. Or, at least, that certainly appeared so to me."

Lord Cathcart looked over my shoulder and smiled.

"If Thérèse wished to discuss horses, she has her wish. But if she wished to keep Bamwell from telling your brother something of interest about King Louis, she has been frustrated. Bamwell and Jack are deep in conversation, and Ferdy is holding forth with Thérèse. Perhaps she is in need of rescue. If you will excuse me."

He nodded and moved off in the direction of Lady Norham.

"Lady Constance!" Althea Sandforth had the air of a cat when a mouse thought to be cornered, escapes under a floorboard.

"Lord Cathcart said something about wishing to speak with Lady Norham, I believe."

"Well, I sincerely doubt that Lady Norham has the bit of news I just this moment learned," Miss Sandforth responded petulantly.

I restrained myself from suggesting that the latest news of the *ton* was not what Lord Cathcart cared to hear from Lady Norham. And my restraint was rewarded, as I was certain it would be, with Miss Sanforth's fresh bit of gossip.

"You will never guess! Major Howells has acquired Lord Poole's estate in Surrey, and plans to restore it to its former luster! Can you imagine the size of the fortune it took just to pay all the mortgages Lord Poole had placed on it? And the sums it will require just to do the basic repairs! Of course, one had heard Major Howells' fortune was sizable, but it must have been even greater than reported!"

"Miss Sandforth, how charmingly animated you are this evening!"

It was Jack in diplomat persona. And beside him was Lord Bamwell, apparently unaware or uncaring that Lord

Cathcart was, at that very moment, engaged in deep conversation with Lady Norham.

"Miss Sandforth, permit me to introduce Lord Bamwell. Bamwell, Miss Althea Sandforth, a true English lady."

Jack did not say, "as opposed to the French Delilah whom you accompanied earlier." But I doubt the message was lost, even on one as dense as Lord Bamwell.

Of course Althea Sandforth and Lord Bamwell were already acquainted, as each admitted. And yet, one had the impression that Jack had purposely thrown each in the way of the other. The brilliance of such a maneuver struck me. In my best matchmaking days, I could not have done better.

The tuning of instruments summoned us back to the music room. Lord Bamwell offered Miss Sandforth his arm, and they sailed forth, to the crescendoing murmurs of the audience as they made their way to the seats that had been previously occupied by Lord Bamwell and Lady Norham. Althea Sandforth now had the look of the cat who licked the cream. But then, so did Jack.

Chapter Thirteen

Undoubtedly, the Hayden piece played after intermission was just as perfect as the Mozart played before intermission, but my brain was too busy to permit me to lose myself in the music. I was almost certain that Jack had deliberately separated Lord Bamwell and Lady Norham. Had he also plotted to foist Lord Bamwell on Althea Sandforth? Or vice versa. And Lord Cathcart had arrived at an amazingly opportune moment, diverting Lady Norham and sweeping her away from the musicale. I could scarcely wait to question Jack on the carriage ride back to Hatton House. But instead of taking his place, after helping Mama and me into the carriage he announced he was off to White's and bid us both a pleasant evening.

The next morning, I retreated to the small sitting room intending to set some perfect stitches and to ferret out what Jack had been up to at Mrs. Beaufort's musicale. When Drusilla Fortesque was announced, I was happy to abandon my stitchery.

A footman bearing a tray of tea and cakes followed close on to Drusilla's arrival, accompanied by an eager Medora, who, in her enthusiasm for a treat, almost tripped the long suffering servant.

"I wanted a quiet evening at home to recoup my forces. I am not as accustomed as you to uninterrupted partygoing, night after night. Do not tell me I missed something vital,"

Drusilla said as she settled herself with the incorrigible Medora on her lap.

"Perhaps not vital, but certainly curious."

I outlined the intricate maneuvers resulting in the separation of Lord Bamwell from Lady Norham, with her subsequent departure with Lord Cathcart and Lord Bamwell's attachment to Althea Sandforth.

"Had I known such an intriguing performance was to be given, I surely would not have missed it," Drusilla murmured regretfully.

"I am certain Jack could enlighten us if he would, but I am just as certain that he will not."

I knew I sounded petulant, but could not help myself.

"Althea Sandforth and Lord Bamwell," Drusilla mused. "Now there is a perfect match if ever I saw one. Such a relief to all the eligible bachelors being pursued by Miss Sandforth, and all the single ladies living in fear of being pursued by Lord Bamwell," she added with her contralto laugh. "Quite an eventful evening for a simple musicale, I must say."

"I almost forgot! There was another bit of news last night. It seems Major Howells has purchased Lord Poole's estate in Surrey."

Drusilla looked up from retying Medora's hair ribbon.

"It is nice to know the major has vast funds at his disposal. He will need them. I understand Lord Poole used the place for his nefarious carryings on and neglected even basic maintenance. But, I confess I would be fascinated to see it for myself."

"What a grand idea!"

I was quite taken by the prospect of a day in the country, exploring the follies and mazes where Lord Poole had disported himself with his raffish friends and the cream of London's demimonde.

Evidently, Drusilla and I were not alone in our enthusiasm to visit Major Howells' newly acquired estate, because the following afternoon, I, and everyone else it seemed, received notes inviting us to be the major's guests at Twin Elms. It was understood the house itself had not been sufficiently renovated to accommodate a party, but a picnic and outdoor activities were proposed. No one sent regrets. Curiosity about the locus of Lord Poole's wild entertainments was universal among the *ton*.

Such an expedition could not be undertaken lightly. Not only did one have to select just the right ensemble, but also a full change of clothing was required in case of misadventure while exploring nature. Cloaks and wraps had to be included in case there was an unfortunate turn of weather. Rugs were necessary for sitting upon. It was obvious that a full complement of servants was essential for the management of all these accoutrements. When I informed Daisy she would be accompanying me on a foray into the country, she was ecstatic.

"Don't worry about a thing, my lady," Daisy reassured me the day before the excursion as I went over the list of items to be included. "I'll take care of everything. I s'pose everyone attending will be needing someone to look after things?"

I agreed absently that most of the invited guests would bring servants with them.

"Will you be traveling to Major Howells' estate with Lord Rochmont, my lady?" Daisy inquired.

I affirmed my intention to do so. Rochmont was driving his curricle, so Daisy would need to travel in a servants' carriage. But even this information did not seem to dampen her spirits.

My final decision, always the most difficult and most important, was what to wear. I settled on an aqua silk organza. That made the jewelry decision easy. Aquamarines were perfect.

Having taken care of this last detail, I felt I could relax and look forward to the visit to Twin Elms. And, honestly, it was good that I could relax, because Daisy was becoming more and more excited as the hours passed. I felt a twinge of guilt and tried to be charitable. Poor thing had been trapped in the city for months. Her eagerness to breathe fresh country air was clearly interfering with her ability to remember her duties as a lady's maid.

"Daisy! Not the yellow muslin, the aqua organza!"

"I'm that sorry, my lady!" Daisy apologized as she pulled a green-sprigged white muslin from the wardrobe.

And so it went. Pearls and peridots were fetched before aquamarines were found. Lavender gloves were returned to the glove box and white gloves were fetched. A braid was started before I reminded her that I wished my hair be arranged in a psyche knot.

"Are you certain you are feeling well enough to make the journey, Daisy?" My question was based in genuine concern for her wellbeing, but her crestfallen look told me how cruel it would be to deny her a longed-for treat. I felt like the worst sort of ogre and did my best to reassure her I had no intention of leaving her behind.

Fortunately, the major packing had been completed the day before, or heaven knows when we would have departed. Medora added to the general confusion, growling and snapping at various boxes and trunks and nipping at the footmen's heels.

Finally, Daisy was able to fasten me into my gown, the correct gloves and bonnet were found, and I descended the stairs. Daisy followed carrying Medora, whose topknot was secured with an aqua bow.

Rochmont greeted me with a smile and a brief kiss upon my cheek and not a word of complaint for having to wait. No wonder he had an endless supply of female admirers. Imagine not being reproached for tardiness! So, as we made our way toward his curricle, I was daydreaming about what life with Lord Rochmont might be, if, indeed, he could come to truly care for me.

I vaguely noted a man I assumed to be a groom, bent

over the front right hoof of a carriage horse. Then he straightened, and I had an instant to record his face—remarkable for its ugliness. It was sallow and pockmarked. But worse was a scar that ran from forehead to jaw. A black patch spared one the sight of what was clearly the ruination of his right eye. The whole was framed by coarse, straight black hair. Scarcely had I registered this picture, when I heard a deep sigh from Daisy, and a white streak that was Medora, ran toward the waiting carriages, alarming the horses, sending gentlemen, manservants and grooms rushing to calm the frightened beasts before anyone or anything was hurt.

Amidst all the confusion, I saw the ugly man, dressed, I noted, in the plain black attire of an upper servant, calmly retrieve Medora, take Daisy by the arm, tenderly settle her in the carriage reserved for servants, and restore Medora to her care. He then addressed Rochmont in a rapid-fire, informal French that I could not begin to comprehend, showing none of the deference usually accorded by a servant to a master. Horses and harnesses were checked and found to be unharmed. Rochmont helped me up to the curricle seat. The servant took the reigns of the carriage where Daisy waited, and we were off.

We drove for some time in silence before I trusted myself to speak. Rochmont obliged me by pretending a need to concentrate on the task of guiding the team safely across the bridge and out of town. But as I glanced at him surreptitiously from under the brim of my hat, I detected a self-satisfied glint in his eyes that erased the gratitude I had previously felt when he had kindly refrained from mentioning my tardy appearance.

We left the city and traveled for some time through the countryside, but the silence between us continued unbroken. I hazarded a glance at Rochmont, and he smiled benignly.

"I do not believe I told you how exceptionally lovely you look today, my dear. I vow the color you are wearing at any given time convinces me it is the one which suits you best."

"That was rather beastly of you, you do know!" I blurted, completely ignoring his well-turned compliment.

Rochmont blinked, but otherwise betrayed no surprise at my outburst. Nor had he altered his grip on the reigns, for the horses betrayed nothing in the way of a change of gait.

"I apologize, Constance. It was inexcusable for me not to present Armand to you. But I confess to having been somewhat preoccupied, what with needing to settle the horses."

In fact, it was a blessing that he had not presented his servant to me. My shock at Armand's appearance had been too strong for me to acknowledge an introduction without embarrassing myself. And I suspected that Rochmont's awareness of that fact was what had kept him from observing the social niceties rather than any preoccupation with the horses.

"That is not what you were beastly about, Rochmont, and you well know it!"

I was too cross to match his tone of light banter.

He smiled his full, heart-melting smile.

"I take it you are unhappy with me for not enlightening you that Armand is not a slick, mustachioed womanizer?"

"It is galling to think of your laughing at my expense. I trust you did not betray me to Armand."

Rochmont had slowed the horses to a walk. The infuriating man was enjoying himself.

"'Betray' is such a cruel word, Constance," he replied with laughter in his voice. "And quite far afield, too. It is difficult to imagine anything more flattering to Armand than to be called a slick womanizer! It was bad enough to endure his being lovesick. But then, when I informed him of your concern about poor, naïve Daisy being seduced by a heartless French rake, his inflated self-esteem was almost too much to bear! He, by the way, would walk barefoot over hot coals to do your bidding, he is so agreeably disposed toward your assessment of his romantic prowess."

"I suppose I can forgive your amusement at my expense, if Armand has made life difficult for you in the process."

"Actually, Constance my dear," Rochmont's voice took on a warm tone that turned my bones to jelly. "While I confess to being amused, I was deeply impressed with your concern for Daisy's welfare. It could not have been easy for you to broach the subject of Armand's behavior with me. We might have been betrothed, but we scarcely knew each other."

Some things had not changed.

"Who else was there to look after the poor girl's best interest?"

I could hear huskiness in my voice that owed nothing to my protectiveness of Daisy and everything to Rochmont's approval of it.

"There was no one else, and you were right to be concerned, Constance. But I assure you that your fears are without grounds. You saw for yourself how it is with both Armand and Daisy."

I did not wish to dwell on my maid's happiness in love and sought to turn the subject.

"You know Armand well, then? I must say he was noticeably lacking in deference toward you."

Rochmont chuckled and returned his attention to the road.

"Uncomfortable with a little *egalite* and *fraternite*, my sweet? Truth to tell, Armand is much more than just a servant. When I ran away and I got myself hired as a cabin boy, I had the presence of mind to introduce myself as Blaise Greeno, but I had not perfected the guttersnipe patois that went with my assumed identity. Armand was a member of the crew. He guessed my background. And even though he was as belittling of me as anyone on the ship, the few times I was actually in danger, Armand would materialize, and the danger would be neutralized."

"Is that how he lost his eye?"

"That was later, in a particularly insalubrious quarter of

Fez. Fortunately, by that time I had the wherewithal to hire the local equivalent of an apothecary."

"Or he would not have survived," I added.

"Probably not."

"It seems so unlikely," I said, puzzled.

"A friendship between Armand and me? I suppose so. But war and chaos are stern schoolmasters in the lessons of loyalty and trust. Armand had witnessed the guillotining of some youthful and obviously innocent children of the aristocracy. He knew my story without my telling it. And his own sense of justice and decency pushed him to do what he could to see that a lamb such as I was not led to the slaughter."

"I meant, Armand and Daisy. They seem so unlikely as a couple."

"I suppose they do." Rochmont caught my eye, a twinkle in his. "But have you never heard of love at first sight?'

I stared at him, seemingly mesmerized, my heart thrumming, my face uncomfortably warm. His gaze lowered to my mouth, which I realized was slightly opened. How mortifying! Gaping like a simpleton! I closed my lips in a prim line.

Rochmont chuckled as he turned the curricle into the gates of Twin Elms. I took care not to meet his glance as he lifted me down. I did not wish to see him notice my flush in response to the strength of his hands on my waist.

"Lady Constance! Lord Rochmont! How perfectly marvelous you both look!"

Never had I been so happy to hear the whispery voice of Lady Antony, who looked quite marvelous herself in white muslin sprigged in embroidered violets. Her hat was an amusing little bonnet adorned with silk violets perched on her glossy black hair. Amethysts sparkled at her ears and neck. I had not seen her more radiant, and told her so.

"How kind of you to say so, Lady Constance. I vow I do thrive in the country air. At heart, I do prefer the quiet of nature."

She gestured prettily to the surrounding lawns and shrubbery, which reflected recent mowing, pruning and sheering.

"Just a simple country girl, at heart," Rochmont agreed blandly.

"You always were uncommonly perceptive, my lord," Lady Antony responded in her childlike tones, glancing up at him through long dusky lashes.

I stifled an urge to administer a sharp kick to the lovely Lady Antony and turned my attention to our host who was approaching.

"Major Howells! How did you achieve this perfect miracle in so brief a time? One had heard, of course of the Herculean task that faced you, bringing some order to the chaos left by Twin Elms' previous owner. I vow, it is well on its way to becoming a veritable paradise."

The major had the grace to blush at my effusions.

"Too kind of you, Lady Constance. But then, your generosity of spirit is known to all."

The gentlemen exchanged greetings, and Lady Antony suggested we discover the vista afforded from the terrace. Major Howells offered her his arm. Rochmont and I fell in behind them.

"Anytime you wish to try outrageous flattery on me, feel welcome to do so," my escort whispered.

"Is there not some sporting event or masculine pastime you wish to pursue?" I asked, trying not to show my amusement.

"I might just do that, as soon as I have enjoyed a vista of this miraculous paradise from the terrace," was his retort.

Before I knew it, Rochmont and Major Howells were discussing the quality of fishing to be had in the nearby streams and had excused themselves so Major Howells could show Rochmont where he intended to shore up the bank of a stream that had been eroded during the spring rain.

But Lady Antony and I were not bereft of companionship. The terrace was a meeting place for almost everyone one knew. Mama, Louisa Fortesque, Maria Canfield-Gould and

Lady Redell, like four monarchs, were arrayed on individual sofas, which Major Howells had thoughtfully caused to be arranged for their comfort. Armies of servants ran to and fro, doing their bidding, fetching parasols, shawls, stitchery, tea, cakes, footstools, rugs, or whatever else it might occur to the queenly quartet that they might require.

Years of practice made it possible for them to give orders, converse, and survey every detail of what was going on anyplace in the wide sweep of the vista before them. They might not see over the tall hedges of the maze, but they would know, at a given instant, just who had entered the maze and who had exited. They might not be able to see into the depths of the spinney, but all four matrons would know to the minute who had spent time there and with whom. Mama had actually brought her opera glasses, professing to be an avid bird-watcher.

Having assured herself that her great aunt was as settled and content as she was capable of being, Drusilla strolled leisurely over to where Lady Antony and I stood. Her gown was of a lighter shade of green than she was accustomed to wear, and along with her chip straw bonnet, it gave her a positively youthful air. Lady Antony noticed the effect.

"Why, Miss Fortesque," Lady Antony greeted Drusilla in her little girl voice. "How charming you look! I vow, every time I see you, you appear lovelier. You must be on the alert for signs of jealousy of ladies not so fortunate, but some of us would be content to learn your secret."

"No wonder you are universally admired, Lady Antony, you are so generous with your compliments." Drusilla's voice sounded quite husky in contrast with Lady Antony's childlike tones. "The only secret I have is one that you have already discovered: a clever modiste and a skilled hairdresser!"

"Is that a fact, Miss Fortesque?" Jack had appeared, seemingly out of thin air. "Whatever gave me the impression you are a veritable repository of surprises, if not actual secrets?"

I felt a *frisson* of concern for my friend. Intelligent and levelheaded she was, but sufficiently so to deal with my charming scoundrel of a brother?

"You must not pay too much attention to Jack's flights of fancy, Miss Fortesque," I advised, hoping desperately to signal a warning to my friend and a reprimand to my brother.

But Drusilla failed to receive my warning, and Jack, as usual was impervious to a reprimand.

"Whatever could have given you the idea I would harbor any secret?" Drusilla's voice sounded positively sultry. She raised her cat-like eyes to Jack's disarming gaze.

He was wearing his sincere little boy look. I was almost ill with concern for my friend.

"Why, close observation, of course."

Jack's look and manner was asking Drusilla to believe in spite of his flitting from lady to lady, he had actually been covertly interested in *her*. I had seen his act too many times not to recognize it.

Drusilla laughed huskily.

"Flattering as being the object of your close observation might be, Captain Hatton, you really will have to come up with some more convincing rationale for your professed belief that I am as devious as you imply."

"Clearly, more time in your company is required before I can rightly claim the scope of understanding I thought I had. Would you care for a stroll about the grounds, Miss Fortesque?"

I stood by helplessly as Jack offered his arm and Drusilla accepted with a graceful nod. As they floated away across the terrace, Jack had the effrontery to turn and wink at me.

"You really need not be that concerned, Lady Constance." I had completely forgotten Lady Antony's presence.

I wanted her to be right.

"Do you believe my worries are for naught?"

"Your brother is not truly ruthless. And Miss Fortesque is no naïve miss. One can never tell in matters of the heart, Lady Constance."

A small smile played on Lady Antony's rosebud mouth. Jack had ignored the real repository of secrets and surprises.

Our respective escorts returned, and I accepted Rochmont's invitation to stroll about the grounds. But if I had expected him to suggest something as romantic as exploring the maze, I was to be disappointed. Rather, we walked through the various gardens, stopping to chat with friends and acquaintances. I spied Althea Sandforth and Lord Bamwell too late to avoid them. But for once I was spared extended conversation, for Miss Sandforth had focused the considerable intensity of her attentions on her companion, and was not interested in wasting time that could better be spent impressing him with her eligibility as a prospective wife. Lord Bamwell's usual hearty address was also missing. He wore a bemused look. Apparently the change in fortunes from vainly pursuing reluctant ladies to being so avidly pursued was a little disorienting.

"Now there is a couple that was destined to be," Rochmont declared as soon as they were out of earshot.

"Perhaps," I acknowledged, "but destiny received major assistance from none other than my brother Jack."

"Indeed. It is difficult to picture Captain Hatton in the role of matchmaker."

We settled ourselves on a bench in the shade of a rose arbor, and I found myself recounting the events of the evening of the Beaufort musicale. I must admit I have never had a more patient listener than my fiancé.

I began by telling him of my surprise at Jack's escorting Mama and me that night.

"I am not at all certain Jack had ever before graced a musicale with his presence. That type of entertainment is not to his liking. And instead of being grateful, as she should have been, Mama spent the entire journey to the Beaufort's door scolding him for his companion and costume the night before.

"But she need not have worried about Jack becoming entangled with Lady Norham, because who should make a grand entrance but the flame-haired lady herself with none other than Lord Bamwell in tow. You can imagine the buzz of reaction by the appearance of *that* twosome."

Rochmont nodded encouragingly, and I continued.

"During the interval, Jack and I encountered Lord Bamwell and Lady Norham. Lord Bamwell was nattering on about King Louis not being up to his royal duties, and Lady Norham kept trying to change the subject. Jack clearly wanted to hear what Lord Bamwell had to say, and Lady Norham was so determined to change the subject, she summoned Ferdy Courlan over to talk about horses."

"That was desperation on Thérèse's part," Rochmont murmured. "So, was her maneuver successful?"

"Not at all. Jack managed to detach Lord Bamwell and I excused myself as Ferdy was beginning to give Lady Norham a horse by horse accounting of his purchases from Lord Poole's stables. Lady Norham looked ready to commit violence against both Jack and Lord Bamwell."

Rochmont laughed appreciatively. "It seems I missed the best entertainment that evening."

"You did, indeed," I assured him, "But it gets even more interesting. About that time, Lord Cathcart arrived, and I told him about Lord Bamwell's conversation with Jack and Lady Norham's efforts to stop it. In an instant, Lord Cathcart had swooped up Lady Norham, and they left together by way of the terrace. Then Jack presented Miss Sandforth to Lord Bamwell and they returned to the music room together. I am certain Miss Sandforth relished being the focus of everyone's attention. Lord Bamwell just looked stunned. Jack looked quite pleased with himself."

I took a deep breath and added a little sheepishly, "The strange thing is, I had the distinct impression that Jack and Lord Cathcart were acting in concert."

"They were."

I was stunned to have my suspicions confirmed.

"I believe I am owed a full explanation." I could hear the steel in my voice.

"I believe you are, indeed," Rochmont admitted. "I was

not free to explain matters that afternoon when you asked. But you have guessed a good deal, and the situation is close to being resolved anyway."

I sat quietly as he gathered his thoughts. Trying to decide how much of the truth to tell me, perhaps? At last he must have decided. He cleared his throat and began his explanation.

"I am sure that you will recall our meeting with Lady Norham in the park."

I nodded. That meeting was impossible to forget.

"At the time, I was certain Lady Norham had come to London to make more serious mischief than just gulling a rich gentleman into replenish her coffers. She had grown up in the émigré circle of the Comte d'Artois, King Louis' younger brother, who is markedly reactionary, even for a Bourbon.

"It is no secret that d'Artois is unhappy with concessions King Louis has made, extending rights beyond the aristocracy in the new French government. D'Artois has always confused his own desires with what is best for France. Or perhaps what is best for France is a question that never enters his mind. Regardless, he has decided the time is ripe to make his move. He is doing his best—or worst, as the case may be—behind the scenes in Paris to discredit and frustrate his brother's government. And he sent the charming Therese to London to cultivate sympathy for his cause and raise funds too. Not for armaments, thankfully, but d'Artois would not want to pay for the necessary bribes from his own pocket. Then there are the costs of printing up inflammatory broadsides and buying cheap wine for street mobs.

"And while the English government is not now and never has been in favor of the tenets of the revolution, it is also quite mindful that an attempt to return to the restrictions and repressions of the *ancien regime* would quite likely serve to inspire another revolution—an event to be avoided if at all possible. So Lady Norham's project had to be frustrated. Right away, I was dispatched to Paris to let King Louis know what was afoot and assess the situation there. Then, of course, Lady Norham's activities needed to be monitored here in London, a task requiring some planning and coordination."

"That afternoon when you and Lord Cathcart were talking with Papa, 'some planning and coordination' were taking place."

I was torn between feeling quite clever for having figured it out and feeling quite dull for not having figured it out sooner.

"Your brother Jack took part too," Rochmont added.

"All part of his new position with the Foreign Office?"

"You must admit your brother has talent for the task."

"And you, you work for Papa, do you not?"

I was trying to discover how I felt about that.

"From time to time I tie up loose ends and find out helpful information for His Majesty's, now Prinny's government. I believe it is the least I can do for a country that provided a safe haven for my mother, my compatriots and me at a time when our lives were worthless in France."

Rochmont looked bleak for a moment, then leaned over and kissed me quickly.

"I do believe that we should see if luncheon is ready. This was to be a picnic, was it not?"

Obviously, he had told me as much as he intended to. I was certain I had more questions, but I felt a surfeit of surprises for one day, and I willingly returned with Rochmont to the terrace, where tables had been set up for luncheon.

But I had not yet had my last surprise of the day. Following dessert, servants appeared with champagne. Major Howells stood and lifted his glass.

"I wish to propose a toast," he said. "To Lady Antony Compton, who has done me the very great honor of agreeing to become my wife."

Lady Antony smiled up at Major Howells beatifically.

Stunned, we all raised our glasses to Lady Antony.

All, that is, except Miss Sandforth, who was whispering in Lord Bamwell's ear.

Lord Bamwell cleared his throat noisily and rose to his feet.

"To Miss Althea Sandforth, who has agreed to become Lady Bamwell."

I looked across the terrace at Jack, who winked at me.

Chapter Fourteen

Standing on the edge of the dance floor, watching others waltzing, was an entirely new experience for me. Not since Countess Lieven had nodded regally, giving me the required permission during my first evening at Almack's, had I been without a partner for a waltz. I had saved this evening's waltzes for Rochmont, who said he would try his best to come to the ball in honor of Althea Sandforth's betrothal to Lord Bamwell. But he had not yet arrived. I reminded myself that it was still early and tried not to feel anxious.

Lord Bamwell was partnering Miss Sandforth—much to the relief of every other lady present. Their performance bore little resemblance to that of Jack's and Drusilla's, whose grace and elegance was punctuated by laughter as they circled the floor while conducting a conversation that clearly amused them both. Major Howells would never match Jack's—or Rochmont's—dancing ability, but he and Lady Antony were the most romantic pair on the floor, circling without speaking, gazing soulfully at each other.

"Er, I know I am a poor substitute, Lady Constance, but if you wish to join the dancers, I would be honored to be your partner."

It was Ferdy Courlan.

"Thank you, Mr. Courlan. You are the most thoughtful of gentleman. But I believe my hairdo is in need of repair."

Ferdy blushed and looked relieved.

I exited the ballroom intending to go to the ladies' retiring room, but instead, I found myself drawn elsewhere—to the library.

I opened the door and gazed at the setting in which my life had taken such a dramatic turn. Nothing in the room had changed—except me. I felt a twinge of loss for the Lady Constance Hatton who had escaped to this library on that fateful night. I strolled over to the looking glass and as I confirmed that the gardenias Rochmont had sent me were still secure above my left ear, I heard familiar voices coming from the hallway. Taking refuge behind a curtain, I carefully checked to be sure that no curl, no flared hem, no ankle or slipper betrayed me.

"So you are quite sure they are safely embarked for France."

The speaker was Papa.

"Not only did I see both Lady Norham and Cathcart board Cathcart's yacht, I waited until it had cast off and made clear of the harbor. I believe we have seen the last of the devious Thérèse for a while," Rochmont assured him.

"I would feel more confident if you had taken the task personally," Papa fretted.

"I am certain Cathcart is the man for the job." Rochmont said confidently. "And, more than that, he is perfectly free and unattached. I think it is time Lady Constance's feelings are taken into account."

They were smoking cigars and I had been fighting the urge to sneeze, but the shock of hearing my own name spoken focused my attention elsewhere quite wonderfully. How dear of Rochmont to be concerned about my feelings! I glowed happily in my hiding place.

"It is good of you to be so thoughtful, Rochmont, ladies do seem to notice that sort of thing. But I cannot say I am in total agreement that Constance needs to be treated with such care. She is a sensible girl. And it is not as if yours is a love match, after all."

Why did Papa have to be so matter of fact about things? I was suddenly close to tears. I wanted Rochmont to protest that he was very much in love with me. But, instead, Papa continued.

"I know you think Cathcart is up to the task, but, after his rivalry with you over Countess Magda, and his overtures to Constance to even the score, I am just a little uneasy about matters."

"I know he regrets that, Lord Chase. You heard him say so. He knew he was out of line making advances to Constance while I was absent. And now that there is no need for rivalry between us anymore, this assignment gives him an excellent chance to prove himself. I believe he will be a very satisfactory replacement for me. I find I am weary of the game. And, as far as Magda is concerned, he is welcome to her."

A tiny glow returned.

"So long as he has this matter with Lady Norham wrapped up before he pursues any other interests," Papa said emphatically. "I suppose there is nothing more to be done until we hear from Cathcart. And I do appreciate all you have done, not just in this little matter, but all the other loose ends you have tied up for us over the years."

"It was an honor to be of service to my adopted country, Lord Chase. I have always believed serving England's best interest also promoted sanity in the country of my birth."

"Thank you for reporting so promptly. At least this time we were able to have a private conversation without unexpected company." Papa chuckled. "I do not believe I was ever more stunned than the last time we were to meet in this very room, and I discovered you here with Constance! I have sometimes wondered why you had not made your escape before I appeared on the scene. Oh well, even the cleverest sometimes slip up. I am promised at the whist tables. You want to come along?"

"Thank you, Lord Chase," Rochmont replied, "but I think I shall finish my cigar and then, I suppose, I shall look for Lady Constance."

The door closed behind Papa, but I remained in my hiding

place, stunned by Papa's revelation. Rochmont certainly must have known Papa would discover us that April evening.

"It is safe to come out now, Constance," I could hear the laughter in Rochmont's voice.

"However did you know . . ."

"The scent of gardenias, Connie. I had already looked in at the ballroom and you were not there."

Rochmont studied my gown, and motioned with his cigar.

"That color quite suits you, my dear. Much warmer and brighter than the usual insipid pink. What is it called?"

"According to Madame Yvette, it is *Rose de Coeur*."

"It requires diamonds, to really set it off, though. Quantities of diamonds," Rochmont decreed, narrowing his eyes judiciously and drawing deeply on his cigar.

"Unfortunately, I do not possess quantities of diamonds."

I did not bother to disguise my irritation.

"I daresay this time next year, you will."

Rochmont's voice was silky and his eyes were warm and compelling. I knew in a moment I would be in his arms and my wits would dissolve. I made myself step away from him.

The warmth left Rochmont's eyes, but his voice betrayed no vexation.

"I would have thought you had all your questions answered quite satisfactorily, Connie. You must realize by now that I am a pretty reliable fellow."

He frowned and rubbed his forehead with the heel of his hand, and then apparently found an explanation for my coldness.

"You are not still ruffled about that little scene between Lady Antony and me in Green Park, are you? You must understand how entirely innocent it was. She wanted to know my opinion of Major Howells. When I told her not only did I believe him to be a gentleman of unblemished character, but also that his fortune was far greater than even common rumor reported, she threw herself into my arms for pure joy and informed me she meant to marry the man. Naturally, I could not divulge her secret to a soul until Major Howells had made things official."

Rochmont smiled warmly, evidently believing that he had destroyed the last barrier of misunderstanding between us.

I straightened my back, determined to discover the truth while my brain was still in something close to working order.

"You knew Papa would arrive any moment that night . . ."

Rochmont shrugged, his one Gallicism, and looked mildly puzzled for a moment.

"Well, yes. He had heard rumors about the d'Artois faction creating some difficulties . . ."

He stopped speaking, looked searchingly at me, and tossed the stub of his cigar into the fireplace.

"You sound unhappy about my meeting with Lord Chase."

For being the most insightful man I had ever met, Rochmont was being astoundingly obtuse.

"I am perfectly happy for you to meet Papa anytime, anywhere. That is not the point at all!"

I could hear my voice getting higher, and just a little shrill, but I could not stop myself.

"I just want to know—need to know—exactly what Papa asked. Why, when you were expecting him at any moment, did you not escape before he arrived?" I was finally able to catch my breath before I added, "And furthermore, I am quite certain you deliberately kissed me just as he entered the library. That was the *coup de grace* sealing our fates."

I had foolishly thought to put Rochmont on the defensive. Instead, he smiled broadly and pulled me into his arms and kissed me lingeringly.

"Because, Connie, my dear," he punctuated the words with a kiss on my forehead. "I had every intention," he kissed my nose. "Of compromising you." He meant to kiss my lips, but I drew back.

"But why?"

"Only for the most honorable intentions, I am afraid. I meant to marry you."

Rochmont gave the appearance of enjoying himself. But I was becoming more and more confused.

I broke from his embrace and he did not attempt to stop me. I began to pace back and forth in front of the hearth. Nothing was making sense to me.

"At the risk of seeming quite dimwitted, may I ask why, if you were so eager to ask for my hand, you did not simply show a tiny bit of interest in me? Perhaps ask me to dance at a ball? Or take the air with you in the park?"

"And have you lead me a merry chase and try to fob me off on one of your dear friends? No, thank you very much. I never considered it for a moment."

I stopped pacing, trying to make sense of what Rochmont was saying.

"But you could not have known I would be here."

Rochmont laughed.

"No, much as I would like to claim burning passion had led me to follow your every move and that I deliberately followed you here, the truth is, finding you here was very much a surprise. A most pleasant surprise, to be sure."

"And you decided, on the spur of the moment, to stay here with me until Papa arrived and demanded to know your intentions?"

It was farfetched, but it was the only explanation that made sense.

"Precisely." Rochmont was obviously pleased I finally understood. "Actually, I have made just about all of the really important decisions in my life based on a little voice in my head that says, 'this is a smart thing to do.' Or 'back out of this as fast as you are able'.

"So here I found myself with a beautiful, entertaining lady, who had eluded the most eligible suitors of the *ton*. A lady who would make my life a misery if I tried to court her, but whose hand could be had for the asking if I decided I wanted it. I decided I did."

I choked back tears.

"Something like a cargo that could be had cheaply and sold dearly, perhaps?"

I was in his arms in an instant, my face buried in his cravat.

"Connie, Connie," he whispered softly. "I would not expect you to believe I fell in love with you that night. I simply knew you would make the perfect wife—beautiful, clever, and challenging from time to time. If I did not fall in love that night, I certainly was enchanted by you. Never did a man walk more willingly and happily into a marriage trap than I did. I do love you now, you know."

He tucked a large white handkerchief into my hand and led me to the nearest sofa.

"When I started loving you, is difficult to say. I had thought to marry a beautiful, sparkling wife who floated easily in the whirl of society. But even before Lord Chase arrived that night, I began to understand in marrying you, I would be getting much more than I had bargained for. Ironic, is it not? In attempting to avoid the rocky shoals of emotion, I was forced to navigate them. Having to leave you so soon after our engagement was announced, knowing you would be scheming to find a replacement fiancé, suspecting eventually Cathcart would make his move . . ."

He gathered me tenderly into his arms.

"Now," he said firmly, "we really must set a wedding date."

"Sometime next April?" I suggested.

"Is that not a terribly long time to ask Armand and Daisy to wait? It would be too awkward for them to wed before we do," Rochmont pointed out.

"St. Valentines Day would be romantic."

"Of course!" Rochmont agreed. "But the weather is so unreliable that time of year."

"Christmas?"

I was beginning to wonder just what date Rochmont had in mind.

The door to the study opened. There stood Mama.

"Constance!"

Rochmont bowed.

"Lady Constance and I were discussing wedding dates."

Mama beamed.

"We were wondering if a September wedding would leave you with sufficient time for planning," Rochmont lied blandly.

"September would present no problem at all," Mama assured him. "Indeed, I cannot see that August would be impossible to manage. But of course," she smiled at us beatifically, "it is up to the two of you to decide."

The library door shut softly behind her.

Mama was incorrigible. I lowered my eyes for a moment, embarrassed to meet Rochmont's gaze. Then I heard his deep chuckle. He was laughing. My great good fortune to have this remarkable man's love made words difficult. I concentrated on the diamond on my hand that lay trustingly in his.

"I do love you, Blaise."

I looked directly into his eyes, and was almost lost in the tenderness I saw.

"I thought I wanted someone to adore me. But what I wanted was someone I could love. You asked how long the search for true love takes. For me, it took just about five years, but it was well worth every second."

I was stunned to discover I had wrapped my arms around his neck as I spoke. Blaise murmured something in French I could not understand. And I could not ask him to explain because he was kissing me quite thoroughly.

"Connie," his voice sounded raspy, "you really must name a date for our wedding. I find I am incapable of rational thought."

I could not hide my amusement.

"Rational thought and common sense can be vastly overrated," I laughed. "Why not get married in July?"